LITTLE MOMENTS
VOLUMES 1 & 2

Little Moments
Volumes One & Two Compilation
By Megan Derr

Edited by Sasha L. Miller
Cover by Megan Derr

First Edition April 2020

Printed in the United States of America

Little Moments

VOLUMES 1 & 2

MEGAN DERR

Table of Contents

Miscommunication

SPELLWEAVER

Johan looked up from the papers he was skimming as his office door opened. Only one person would dare to enter without knocking, and sadly it wasn't his lovely young lover looking for an afternoon tryst.

He smiled anyway, and set down his papers, rising to bow in greeting. "Your Highness."

Prince Trisar scoffed as always at Johan's manners, the gold thread in his lace cuffs and at his throat glinting in the afternoon sunlight. "Are you busy?"

"Never too busy for you," Johan replied with a smile.

Most of the royal family was far too serious for their own good, leaving Prince Trisar the very odd one out. He was the size of a house and built like a fortress, but where his family all dressed like they expected to attend a funeral at any given moment, Trisar's style had more in common with a boudoir. Or a cake.

They'd been friends from the moment they'd met as boys, Johan hiding from doing yet another pile of syrup-sticky dishes, Trisar sneaking off with some of his sisters' old dresses to try on.

He wasn't wearing a dress today, though his thigh-length jacket could nearly pass for one of the scandalously short dresses the people on Lovers' Lane wore to draw in customers. It was dyed in purple ombre, with a delicate, barely visible swirl of silver roses and vines. His long, long black hair was bound up in an elegant twist and decorated with purple roses, and amethysts dripped from his ears and gleamed on his fingers.

The only contrast to the ensemble were the green gloves he wore, precisely like Johan's. The second child of the royal family—the spare, as people loved to call him—it was Trisar's duty to oversee magic, ensure the laws were obeyed, violators suitably punished, and so forth.

As a child, Johan's aspirations had been no greater than getting a job away from the kitchen—maybe something as lofty as head footman. But after he'd accidentally become Trisar's best friend, he'd been drawn into the world of magic and proven to have a knack for it—a knack the queen had not wanted overlooked.

And now he was the second most powerful magic user in the kingdom. Only the Lord Breaker, Kirra, was stronger than him, and Trisar was a very close third. Kirra handled the broader aspects of the job—international tangles, mostly, and some of the thornier and more delicate matters involving nobles. Johan dealt with local problems, and everyone not a noble.

Trisar smiled. "I need your advice on an important matter."

"Intriguing." Johan shoved away from the desk and walked with him out of the office and through the halls, until they came to one of the more remote courtyards—not private, per se, but enough of a walk that few people bothered to use it unless specifically ordered or invited to be there.

Currently, it looked as though it had been set up for some private little gathering, where people could meet one another, chat for a time, nibble on sweets and such. Johan hated them, and avoided them as much as he possibly could. More often than not, he sent one of his secretaries or warlocks to stand in for him—they enjoyed the chance to make powerful connections, he enjoyed being able to get real work done.

"Who do we have here, then?" he asked, brows lifting, because it wasn't hard to pick out the three princes and solitary princess in the mix, and the ten or so people who comprised their various entourages. "What's being negotiated today, and why would I have any useful advice?"

"My marriage," Trisar said with a sigh. "I'm to pick one of the four by the end of the month, or else my mother will do the choosing herself, and frankly I'd rather go about naked the rest of my life. Everyone else can rattle off the political reasons I should marry; I'd like your non-political input."

Johan laughed briefly at the idea of Trisar forsaking clothes, then sobered and gave the candidates a more thorough going over. The princess seemed… well, honestly, a lot like Trisar. In demeanor and dress they could have been siblings, though her skin was moonglow pale and her hair the color of rubies. "I'm not sure you and the princess would get along in the child-making way, which I'm sure is an expectation piled upon her."

"Oh, quite," Trisar replied. "She's a lot of fun, but every time I think about kissing her, I feel vaguely ill, like I'm getting amorous with a sister or cousin. She feels the same. I suppose alcohol and determination would get us through the matter, but why make us both miserable? Still, she's honestly the least depressing of the lot."

"Interesting," Johan said. "What about the dark, brooding one in the corner? He's beautiful."

Trisar sighed, eyes falling on the man in question, and he looked for a moment deeply sad. "Arran. Smart, good leader, would be bringing an alliance with Kartermine with him, and a personal connection to the Sharmora, which is worth a kingdom all on its own. But he hates me; every time we're in the same room he glares so hard I fear I'll catch on fire. No idea what I did to earn his contempt, but I have enough of it for three of me. A pity, because I'm told he's perfectly lovely, if somewhat stand-offish, when I'm not around."

"Hmm..." Johan said thoughtfully. "What about the remaining two?"

Before Trisar could reply however, two more people came into view, new arrivals to the private fete. Happiness burst in Johan's chest and spread through his body as he watched Myka, who practically clung to Lady Sartin out of terror as she introduced him to some of the local nobility in attendance, as well as the visiting royals.

"He's a darling," Trisar said with another sigh. "I wish someone looked at me the way you and Myka look at each other."

Johan was fairly certain that given half a chance, Trisar would look at Arran in such a way, but he forbore comment—and then forgot, as sharp, cutting words filled the clearing and one of the foreign princes gave Myka a ringing slap.

"I beg your pardon!" Trisar bellowed, and all heads immediately turned and snapped up, dozens of eyes filling with horror as everyone realized the man of the hour had quietly been watching them for who knew how long.

Trisar grabbed the edge of the balcony, swung neatly over it, dropped to hang from the edge, and then smoothly dropped to the ground.

Johan lifted his eyes to the sky, but at the curt jerk of Trisar's head, deftly repeated the ridiculous maneuver. Gods knew they were old hands at doing stupid things in and around the palace, though leaping balconies had been easier when he was twenty.

"Myka," Johan said softly, crossing over to him and pulling him close. He gently grasped Myka's chin in one green-gloved hand, and tilted his head to get better look at the mark that was already bruising.

"Is he all right?" Trisar asked.

Johan let Myka go with a soft kiss. "Are you?"

"I'm fine," Myka said. "But I wish someone would explain to me why I got slapped. I didn't mean to cause offense."

Trisar barked out several sharp words at the man who'd slapped Myka. A few minutes later, the man looking muchly withered, Trisar said, "He took something you said as a massive insult, instead of remembering how often he himself has cast insult without intending it, because most of us can't communicate clearly in our own language, let alone others."

The prince said something else, and Trisar added, "He says he is sorry, and offers a full length of spelled Termion linen in apology."

Johan glanced briefly at Trisar, recognizing the look in his eyes. The man was offering no such thing, if he had to guess, but he'd hear about it at some point, and realize just how mad Trisar really was.

Well, that was two candidates firmly

down.

The prince slunk off, his entourage close on his heels, and the rest of the party broke up almost immediately after, everyone eager to avoid causing more trouble—or more likely, eager to spread gossip.

Only Prince Arran lingered, and the look on his face—surprise, intrigue, and more than a little want—had Johan dragging Myka away, leaving Trisar and Arran alone.

Holding to Myka's hand, he led the way through the palace to the gardens, pausing only to have a maid fetch him some ointment from the palace healer. When that had been brought, he led Myka to the gazebo where they'd first dallied, during the royal ball when he'd thought Myka some passing stranger he'd never see again, without no clue his companion was really the spell weaver he'd pined and lusted after for months.

Myka shot him an amused look as he took a seat. "I'm not sure I trust your motives in bringing me here."

Johan laughed. "What's not to trust? Even if I had brought you here for a tryst, wouldn't you enjoy that?"

"True," Myka said with a laugh of his own. It vanished beneath a slight wince as Johan began to treat his bruised cheek. "I hope I haven't caused any trouble. Lady Sartin was showing me around, and introduced me to Prince Westen because we import so many valuable fabrics from his country."

"It takes more than accidentally calling some royal brat a mangy dog, or whatever he was griping about, to ruin trade agreements. Trust me. If one insult from a spell weaver was enough to cause that kind of rift, the wars would never stop."

Myka moaned and covered his eyes with his fingers. "I can't believe I said that. I practiced my greetings all week!"

Johan chuckled, and pulled his hands away, kissing the knuckles of both. "Beloved, I have enough stories of offensives I've caused—accidentally *and* on purpose—to fill a library. Trisar doesn't consider his day well spent unless he'd offended at least one person. Everyone from Their Majesties on down to the lowliest kitchen boy manages to offend some royal or noble at least once a week. As long as you don't strike them or something, very few people in the palace mind, and those who do mind are ignored."

"I suppose," Myka said, cuddling close when Johan pulled him in, seeming soothed by the kiss Johan dropped on his mouth. "I'm not sure I'm cut out for palace life."

"You're doing marvelously, and you'd realize that if you stopped fretting." Johan stroked his back soothingly, lingering every now and again to tease the back of his neck, eliciting lovely shivers. "Everyone I speak with mentions to me how lovely you are—in deed and in looks." He winked. "I think a few are pouting that I scooped you up before they ever knew you existed. I'm not terribly sorry." That got the laugh he'd been hoping for. "Have you gone into the city yet, today?" Johan asked.

"No, I was going to go after the party."

"Do you mind if I tag along? Incognito, of course." If he wore his green gloves anywhere near Ash Street, people would run and hide. So many in the poor districts were precisely as Myka had been: struggling, unlicensed, harassed by slum lords, and half a step away from being arrested for things that ultimately were not their fault.

That was the very last thing Johan wanted, especially since Myka went there to help out his old friends and neighbors. He drew a paycheck now that was, according to him, more in a month than he tended to earn in at least two years.

And instead of spending it, or saving more than a small sum of it, Myka gave it away to help out others. If Johan hadn't already been in love after the past several months together, he probably would have fallen in love at just that.

It also made him want to do more himself to help, though his methods were more general and sweeping, as he simply didn't have the time to do it Myka's much more personal way.

Soft lips brushed his cheek. "Shouldn't you be working, not out here soothing and cozying up to me in hopes of a gazebo tryst?"

"I only sought to soothe, I promise," Johan said with a smile. "Tempting though you always are, even I would get in no small amount of trouble for being caught behaving so in the middle of the day. Very few in this place want to see that much of me."

Myka laughed. "I think the numbers might surprise you."

Johan pinched his nose, then kissed him. "It's the green gloves and the fact I call Trisar by his name, more than anything. I've only known one person to nearly pass out in terror because of who I am." He chuckled when Myka made a face. "So about a tryst…"

"Oh, no," Myka said, though he laughed again. "Lady Sartin is probably looking for me, and I know you have work aplenty. You can wait until tonight."

"Fine," Johan said with a sigh, pouting as he stood. He drew Myka into his arms and kissed him properly—long and deep and full of delightful promise. "But I expect it to be worth my wait, Your Highness."

"Hahaha," Myka retorted. "Isn't it always?"

Johan kissed him again in reply, and added in a bit of fondling that got him a startled squeak. "See you later then." He sauntered off, laughing at Myka's flustered shouting, as it would probably be a few minutes before he was fit to leave the gazebo.

Whistling, Johan headed back to his office.

Basking

BACKWOODS ASYLUM

Was there anything better than basking?

Well, yes. The three puppies sleeping off their forays into the pond, and the handsome man who would be joining them eventually. But sprawling on his rock and soaking up the sunshine, with nothing before him but a weekend with his family at his house in the woods, was a close second to those dual firsts.

Skylar smiled faintly as he heard the soft rustle of someone trying to approach unnoticed. "You can't think you're really going to sneak up on me on my own turf."

"I wouldn't even bother trying," Brady said with a warm laugh. "I just didn't want to bother you. I was also admiring the view. Whenever you talked about basking on your rock, I stupidly assumed clothes were involved."

Brady sat down next to him, resting a cool hand on Skylar's heated skin, and Skylar finally opened his eyes and stared into Brady's beautiful green-yellow ones. "Silly you. What's the point of basking if you have all those clothes in the way? They just get sweaty and itchy."

"Silly me," Brady said, skimming a hand lightly along his torso. "Cruel you, looking like this when there are children nearby and I can't do all the things I'm thinking about."

Skylar laughed and sat up, reaching for his clothes. "Help me carry them home and maybe we can steal a couple of hours to ourselves."

"Well I suppose that's a suitable trade for my promised afternoon of swimming and sunbathing," Brady replied with a smile, and reeled him for a nice, long kiss that tasted faintly of chocolate.

"Someone's been in my candy jar," Skylar said as he pulled away.

Brady just grinned as he took Skylar's hand, weaving their fingers together, even though the pups were a short distance away. It was just one of the many little things he did that Skylar loved about him. Sometimes, he wondered how on earth he'd ever thought Brady hated him.

As they reached the little pile of sleeping puppies, Brady kissed the back of his hand before letting go, then knelt and scooped up Hansel and Gretel, who were big enough now that Skylar couldn't easily carry them both anymore. Instead, he picked up a snuffling Annabelle—Bella—and cuddled her close. The twins were plenty capable of shifting, had been for the past couple of months, but Annabelle was little enough she couldn't yet manage it. To keep her company, and because they could move more easily with four legs, the twins generally stayed in wolf form.

The hike back to the house was quiet, save for the rustle of animals and a chorus of birdsong. Throughout, the pups didn't so much as stir, save for Hansel, who mumbled sleepily in that 'I want cookies' way of his before falling silent again.

Once the twins were in their bed, because they refused to sleep separated, and Bella was in her crib, Skylar headed back down the hall to the living room, followed a moment later by Brady.

His phone promptly went off, making them both groan.

Skylar loved being a father, even more than he'd thought he would. Better still, he had a partner, when he'd always assumed he'd be a single parent.

But jeez did he hate being a famous parent. Ever since the media and everyone else had gotten wind of the adoption, his weeks had been filled with interviews, requests to give speeches, luncheons, banquets, and more—everybody wanted to talk to him, or listen to him, or ask for his help.

It wasn't that he minded, he was all for being an advocate for the kinds of changes that allowed people to adopt whatever child they loved, regardless of shifter species. He was definitely enjoying people not being scared of him, though there would always be assholes who called him feral, half-wild, and worse.

He wouldn't mind a break, though. More time to focus exclusively on his family. He and Brady had been together nearly a year now, though sometimes it felt like they'd always simply *been.* How, he didn't know. He kept waiting for Brady to get sick of him, for them to find some issue on which they clashed. But all they'd dealt with was the usual minor scuffles of learning to live together and adjust their individual habits, and the occasional meltdown from all the stress on them because of the adoption.

They'd gotten so busy, Brady had hired a personal assistant to help them manage it all. She was the one who'd finagled this break for them. "I thought I turned that stupid thing off," Skylar said, and went to go do so for real this time, not even bothering to look at who it was. He had specific tones set up for family and friends, and the ringtone had been the generic one for everybody else.

Once it was definitely off, he threw it back on the armchair and turned to Brady, hands sliding into the back pockets of his jeans as he admired the view of Brady approaching. "Now, then, where were we?"

Brady swept him up and nipped playfully at his lips, before taking his mouth and pushing his tongue deep, tasting and claiming, leaving Skylar shivering. Pulling his hands free, Skylar wrapped his arms around Brady's neck and kissed hungrily back. Between three children and the demands on their time, chances to spend time together just the two of them was rare.

"I believe you were about to take those clothes right back off so I can touch the way I wanted to at the pond," Brady said against his mouth.

Skylar kissed him again, then stepped back and removed his t-shirt, casting it in a nearby chair so his clothes would be easy to locate again. "Are you sure we shouldn't be in the bedroom, if one of them wakes up?"

"I closed the doors; they won't be getting out even if they shift."

"Did you lock our children in their rooms?"

"I took advantage of their lack of stature," Brady said with a snicker. "They won't even notice, and if something goes wrong we'll hear it."

Skylar pulled off Brady's shirt and tossed it to join his, then worked deftly on the button and zipper of his jeans. Brady shuddered as Skylar pulled out his cock and stroked it teasingly. "I can't believe I ever thought you were scared of me, or painfully shy, or anything but pure evil delight." He groaned as Skylar sank to his knees, taking Brady's clothes with him, and it was the work of moments before he had Brady naked and that cock in his mouth. He pulled it in deep, working his throat and tongue, enjoying the musky flavor and scent, the way Brady occasionally lost himself and jerked his hips, thrusting even further into Skylar's mouth, nearly taking away his ability to breathe.

It was heady how easily Brady lost himself when they were like this. None of his few other lovers had ever trusted even half as easily as Brady had right from the start, as easily as he did every single time, no mater what they did. He'd actually seen Skylar attack someone, and still he never worried if Skylar might lose control or something equally stupid and offensive.

Skylar squeezed his hips, and Brady happily heeded the signal, thrusting into his mouth with abandon and moaning Skylar's name as he came.

When he was done, Skylar pulled off his softening cock slowly and wiped his mouth with the back of his hand—and yelped as he was pushed to the floor, right across the faux-fur rug where he'd first cuddled up with Hansel and Gretel, and kissed senseless.

By the time he was permitted to come up for air, Brady was straddling him and taking Skylar's cock in hand. "Guess what I did before heading for the pond?"

Skylar tried to reply, but the words were lost in a loud groan as Brady sank down easily on his cock. "You're such a brat."

"Is that a complaint?"

"Not even close," Skylar gasped out as Brady rode him, lifting up and grinding down hard, taking Skylar's cock like it was his sole purpose. Skylar could do nothing but hold fast to Brady's hips and take it, though that was far from a complaint. He loved best when Brady rode him, fucked himself on Skylar's cock with enthusiasm, riding him until could take no more, moaning his name and coming so hard he saw white.

As he came down, Brady rolled off him and sprawled next to him, turning Skylar's head to kiss him lazily, smelling of sweat and sex. The only thing better was when they all piled together in their big bed and smelled simply like family.

"Hey, cottonmouth," Brady said, nuzzle the crook of his throat. "Come here often?"

"Not as often as I'd like," Skylar replied, pinching him for the stupid pun, laughing when that got him swatted.

Brady licked his throat, eliciting a shiver. "You smell like sunshine and sex." He tugged so it was Brady sprawled on the rug and Skylar was draped across him. "One of my favorite things."

"I can tell," Skylar replied with a snicker at the half-hearted twitch Brady's cock gave. "But I think your other favorite thing will have to wait a bit for round two. Especially since somebody promised me barbeque chicken."

Brady kissed him, hands skimming his body and coming to rest on his ass. "I would never deny you food, especially when I promised it. If I had known food was all it took, I'd have seduced you in college with bread and cookies."

"That definitely would have worked." Skylar stole one last quick kiss, then reluctantly climbed to his feet and retrieved their clothes. "Come on, if you hurry you might get lucky again in the shower." He laughed as Brady rolled to his feet and bolted for their bedroom.

Good Bad Behavior

LOVE YOU LIKE A ROMANCE NOVEL

Jet winced inwardly at the sound of familiar footsteps—a certain pace, the click of Jimmy Choo loafers that were only a week old, replacing the previous pair he'd bought Jason. How buying his lover shoes had become a thing, he didn't quite remember, but though Jason had excellent taste in suits, his taste in shoes was godawful boring. So Jet took care of it.

He slowly dragged his eyes up, looking through the bars at the man watching him, thankfully, with more amusement than anything. "I'm not sure what to ask about first," Jason said, eyes roaming Jet thoroughly. "The shiner, the pattern of that minidress, or why Dai isn't here with you."

"He got sick, couldn't come," Jet said morosely. "I didn't go looking for a fight, you know. I wasn't fucking bothering anyone."

Jason motioned with a nudge of his chin to the nearby officer, who unlocked the door to let

Jet out. "Lucky for you, there are plenty of cameras to prove that. Marden's lawyer is already calling about working something out." As Jet cleared the cell, Jason reeled him and kissed him thoroughly, but carefully, given the bruises on his face and his split lip. "You still have not explained the minidress."

"It's Versace."

"It's rainbow leopard print. Please don't tell me you paid real money for that."

Jet grinned. "No. I modeled it in a magazine shoot, and they let me keep it when the shoot was finished, along with the other clothes I modeled. How do you think I get so many of my nicer pieces?"

"I hope you're not lumping that dress in with 'nicer pieces'," Jason replied. "I assumed you bought them like the rest of the world." He sighed when Jet just curled into his chest, doing a poor job of muffling his laughter. "Brat. Where are your shoes?"

Jet stopped laughing, his shoulders drooping. "I took them off so I could fight. They got stolen. My Dolce & Gabbana pumps."

"The garishly pink ones?" When Jet nodded, Jason smiled and kissed his nose. "You needed a new pair anyway. Come on, let's go home. Thank you, Officer Brook."

He winked and laughed. "Always a pleasure to see Jet."

Once they were done with processing, Jet

followed Jason disconsolately to his car, and curled up in the seat on the way home.

"You're not usually this upset about getting arrested," Jason said, looking at him as they came to a stop light.

Jet shrugged. "I've been trying to behave. I think I've caused us more than enough hassle and grief over the years."

Jason frowned, but said nothing as he resumed driving, and they were quiet the remainder of the trip.

Once inside Jason's house, though, Jet didn't even get a chance to turn the lights on before Jason had him shoved up against the kitchen island, mouth crashing into his, deft hands pushing the dress up to his hips and yanking down the panties he'd worn beneath.

He was forced to tear away to undo the work Jet had done to get his dangly bits up out of the way of the dress, but then he was right back to feasting on Jet ravenously. Jet could only hold on for dear life and enjoy the ride—and what a ride it was, as Jason hitched him up onto the island and spread him wide, tearing open a packet of lube and making quick and dirty work of Jet's hole, trailing sucking kisses and sharp bites along his throat all the while.

Jet moaned as Jason thrust into him a moment later, hot and heavy, stretching and burning oh so wonderfully. He held fast to Jason's shoulders, glitter-painted fingers clinging to fancy wool, desperate for purchase, before he finally gave up and fell back, head knocking a fruit bowl and sending it crashing to the floor. "Jason—"

That got him even harder thrusting, and a hand on his cock, stroking him roughly, making him howl as he came. Jason thrust into him a few more time, then sank in deep and came moaning Jet's name.

Their panting breaths filled the kitchen, ragged and hard, chests heaving. Hair and clothes were completely mussed, and Jet was probably going to have to toss the dress. Not that he was in much of a hurry to keep it, not now that a shitty evening had ruined it. But at least it had gone out with a delightful bang.

"Not that I'm complaining, but what was that for?"

Jason fetched a cloth to clean them up, then gently pulled Jet off the island and set him back on his feet. "Like you aren't well aware how much I like you dressed this way."

"Like Club Night Barbie?" Jet grinned. "I thought the rainbow leopard print offended you."

"Stuck between turned on and offended is a perpetual state with you," Jason retorted. "Stop being upset you got arrested. I only get upset when you get naked in front of people, which you haven't done since we actually got together. Punching transphobic assholes outside a club I own isn't going to upset me. Hell, that's the kind of shit that boosts sales. Not that your band needs the help. But I told that shithead's lawyer we'd talk tomorrow. Dormer will make him suffer."

"Heh." Dormer handled all such matters for Jason's clients, and hiring him had done a lot to increase the awareness and popularity of Jason's firm. A whole bunch of clients had wound up jumping ship when they'd found out Jason left, and despite repeated attempts—many of them ridiculously generous—Jason had no intention of returning to his father's firm.

Jet just liked seeing him so much happier than he'd ever been. "I'm tired."

"After a night of clubbing, punching people, and getting arrested? That's a light evening for you." Jason took his hand and they made their way upstairs."

"And getting fucked within an inch of my life, don't forget that part."

"Wait until we get in the shower."

Well-earned Respite

KISS THE RAIN

Selsor collapsed on the bed with a groan, draping one arm over his eyes to block out the sunlight. Would anyone notice if he called up some clouds? Probably. He sighed and rolled over. Too much heat. Too much sun.

Too much time spent with obnoxious assholes who hadn't changed at all in the years since Selsor's banishment. They'd done everything they could to avoid simply saying *We're sorry. We made a mistake, that mistake cost you the livelihood you should have had and forced you to endure years of abuse and neglect, we will do all we can to make amends.*

On the other hand, they hadn't been able to do anything but grit their teeth and do everything Prince Allanci had "requested" in the letter he'd sent along with Selsor. He'd finally get to finish school, paid in full—room and board included—by the school itself in recompense for their mistakes. *And* he was on a special track just for him, since he didn't need to start in the same place as the new students. In a couple of years, he'd have his papers. In the meantime, he'd be balancing school with helping Jenohn.

Where was Jenohn, anyway? He'd said he'd be home all day. Normally on his days off, he couldn't be torn away from spending time with the local kids.

Groaning again, Selsor heaved to his feet and went to see where his errant… friend? Lover? What were they exactly? Lover most often implied there was sex involved, but there hadn't been any of that.

How had they even come to this when they barely even knew each other?

Yet every time Selsor thought of Jenohn, warmth and wary happiness spread through him. The man he'd nearly killed as a youth was the only person who'd fought for him his whole life, even when Selsor didn't know it. That would never stop awing him.

It didn't hurt Jenohn was a good person, with a golden heart, and… well, Selsor wasn't going to complain if they added sex to their unorthodox relationship.

Heading back downstairs and outside, Selsor followed the sounds of playing children to the small square in their section of housing, which boasted a fountain for drinking water and a second one for laundry. The children had absconded with various bowls and pitchers and were doing their best to drown each other. Given how hot the day was, Selsor thought it the most brilliant idea ever, even if he had nowhere near that kind of energy these days.

They stopped when they saw him, and waved and called out.

"Have you seen Jenohn?" Selsor asked when they quieted, dispensing the sweets he'd taken to carrying around for them.

"Some people showed up and made him mad. He stormed off and they followed," one of the girls said, shrugging. "They should know not to do that. Jenohn is always right, and he doesn't like to get angry."

Selsor didn't roll his eyes, but it was a near thing. "Which way did they go?"

The children pointed as one down a road that led to the guardhouse where Jenohn went to train and pick up small tasks between those given to him by the prince. "Thank you. Don't break those dishes, you'll upset your mothers!"

He headed off, more worried than ever. Who had come from the guardhouse and angered Jenohn? That was actually a really difficult thing to do. Jenohn was unflappable. In the few months Selsor had been living with him, he'd only ever seen Jenohn get peeved a couple of times. And back when they met, he only got angry at the people responsible for the flooding.

Selsor's step slowed despite himself as the gates of the guardhouse came into view. His experience with soldiers was poor at best. They were good at shoving and kicking him out of the way, laughing as they messed up the floor he'd just spent three hours cleaning. Shoving him into walls and demanding with foul breath that he suck their cock, or bend over the nearest table.

Tamping down on his nerves, he set his shoulders, lifted his chin, and strode through the gates. He could call down lightning, he could handle a bunch of stupid soldiers.

A few gave him looks as he walked past, but nobody stopped him. He looked around for someone to question—and stopped as he heard Jenohn's voice crying out in pain. Worry, fear, and anger rushed through Selsor, and as he followed the sounds around the main building to the yard behind it, clouds slowly began to cover the sun.

Turning the corner, he came upon a circle of men standing around a figure lying on the ground. Jenohn. He lifted his head briefly, before he was forced to protect it with his arm. But all Selsor registered was the blood.

"What are you doing!" He bellowed, the wind kicking up around him.

Everyone turned, and familiar, ugly expressions filled the face of the seven—no eight—soldiers who'd been beating Jenohn.

"Who the fuck are you?" the biggest, ugliest one asked, stepping forward, bracing his bloody fists.

"Why are you hurting him?"

Jenohn heaved slowly, painfully, to his feet. "Selsor, don't. I can handle—"

"Shut up," Selsor said. "I'll deal with you in a minute. First I'm dealing with these refuse-eating ballsacks."

They all laughed meanly, and one of the not-quite-as-big ones said, "What do you think you can do to us, mage?"

Selsor called up his magic, and the clouds overhead grew heavier, darker. "Tell me why you're hurting my soldier or you'll find out. He reports directly to Prince Allanci, you must know hurting him is practically a death sentence."

"He won't be working for him much longer, not if he keeps up with that holier-than-thou attitude," said the big one. "He won't be working for anyone if he doesn't learn to keep his mouth shut."

Selsor sighed—then threw out his hands, sending controlled bolts of searing lightning into each and every one of them. Stunned motionless, they were easy pickings then for Jenohn, even as battered and bruised as he was.

When he was finished, Jenohn limped over to him. "Can we go home?"

"I should leave you in whatever ditch you fall into," Selsor said, even as he hooked an arm around Jenohn's waist and settled one of Jenohn's arms over his shoulders. "What is this about?"

"Let's get home first. I don't think I can walk and talk at the same time right now."

Selsor acquiesced, helping him through the streets, gently shooing off the children when they crowded around in concern. Back in their home, he got Jenohn seated in the kitchen and set to work cleaning away all the blood so he could take better stock of the wounds. "Anything internal hurt?"

"Only my ribs, but they're bruised, not broken. I'll be fine with a few days' rest," Jenohn said with a sigh. "How are you? I know you've been practicing that move, but I didn't know you'd perfected it."

"Neither did I," Selsor said. "But there was no other way to make sure I wasn't going to join you in looking like something freshly ground by the butcher. What in the world is going on?"

Jenohn leaned into his touch as Selsor rested hand against his still-oozing temple to heal it, his eyes falling closed. "What is it always?" For a moment, Jenohn looked so weary Selsor thought he might shattered if touched. "I pissed someone off. They used one of our assignments as a ploy, and when I went to speak to the Captain of the Guard about it, hoping I wouldn't have to bother Allanci, they jumped me in the yard."

"What assignment?"

"That prisoner I'm in charge of escorting in a couple of months. They claimed the order to remove us from the team was sent by the king."

"But why do they want to beat you up?"

"Because I caught some of them availing

themselves of the whores on Thicket Street and ratted them out to Allanci, who had all parties that could be proven guilty kicked out of the guard and gang-pressed. Their buddies left behind aren't best pleased with me."

Selsor checked his healed forehead, then knelt to attend his ribs and the gash on his thigh. It left him acutely aware that he was between Jenohn's legs, he was half-naked, and his cock was right there, just as stupidly big as the rest of him.

Forcing his thoughts back to work, he set to healing Jenohn's ribs first. "They must know they'll get worse than gang-pressed for beating *you* up."

"I don't think they really cared at the time. I ruined all their fun, and took their friends away." Jenohn shrugged, and Selsor hated, *hated*, seeing him so downcast. But even Jenohn must grow weary of the way he was treated, no matter how unflappable he always seemed.

Selsor worried his bottom lip, thoughts and ideas tumbling through his mind. "After this escort business, do we have anything important to do? Classes don't start for another month, so I have plenty of time to fill."

"I don't think I have much of anything, actually," Jenohn said. "Allanci is going on his summer retreat soon, and I'm not going with him this time. I was hoping you and I could spend more time together."

Rising, Selsor said, "How do you feel?"

"Huh? Oh, fine."

"Good." Selsor squished all his nerves like they were insects and sat in Jenohn's lap.

Jenohn froze, gawked briefly, then grinned in that adorably bratty way of his and held Selsor fast. "Does this mean I can have a kiss?"

"When have I ever told you not to kiss me, you oaf?"

Chuckling, Jenohn trailed his lips whisper soft across Selsor's cheek, then teased at his lips briefly before giving a proper kiss. Selsor didn't know who he had to thank for Jenohn's skills, but he was obscenely grateful. The man kissed like he'd put as much effort into mastering it as he'd put into his combat skills. His lips were soft, his mouth warm, tongue sweeping and commanding as he plundered Selsor's mouth at his leisure. He kissed like there was nothing else in the world he wanted to do.

Selsor wanted that to be true for a very long time.

Eventually drawing back, he stroked Jenohn's short hair with his fingers, cupping the back of his head and digging nails in just the way Jenohn liked, pressing his forehead to Jenohn's temple. "So what do you say to going away for a month? Somewhere quiet, where we can just be, without all this muss and fuss around us. You've waited a long time to find me; seems a shame you never get to see me, except when we're working."

Jenohn's face lit up like the sun coming

from behind storm clouds. "I know just the place!"

"I'm going to guess it belongs to Allanci and he lets you and the others use it whenever you like," Selsor said with a smile.

Jenohn poked him in the ribs. "Brat. But yes. His hunting lodge. We use it more than he does, I swear. I'll go see him and make the arrangements. There will be a basic staff there, but otherwise it'll be just us."

"Sounds perfect," Selsor said, and reluctantly slid off his lap—but not complaining when Jenohn drew him into a breathless kiss. "I think I know just what we'll do when we get there."

That got him pushed into the wall and kissed ravenously. He pushed Jenohn away after several wonderful, agonizing minutes. "Go do your part, and I'll let the school know they get a month's reprieve."

Jenohn grinned, kissed his cheek, and raced off.

~~*

The hunting lodge was more like a hunting palace, but that didn't exactly shock Selsor. "Is this much house really essential to slaying animals?"

"A royal hunt is more like a two week binge of eating, drinking, sleeping, drinking, fucking, and drinking. There may be one or two token attempts at hunting, where mostly they ride horses at unwise speeds and let the huntsmen do all the real work. Allanci doesn't care for them, so he only does it when his father insists."

"Rich people are stupid."

Jenohn laughed as he dismounted, and then helped Selsor down, holding him close and giving him a long, thorough kiss. "You do realize we work for one of the richest?"

"Allanci somehow managed to escape the gross stupidity and buffoonery of his peers. I don't know how, but I actually like him."

"Hmm," Jenohn said. "Do I need to be jealous?"

Selsor laughed. "As though I could compete with his bodyguards. But no, I'm quite happy with my soldier, even if he is a know-it-all brat."

That got him another kiss, a delightful slow-burn, sweet and thorough and mind-melting. He didn't know how this man had gotten so deeply under his skin, but he wasn't sorry about it.

When they finally drew apart, he asked, "So are you going to show me to our bedroom, or did you just want to fuck in the hallway?"

"I don't think the servants should be forced to endure that," Jenohn replied with a grin. "They put up with enough during the royal hunts." He stepped back, took Selsor's hand, and practically dragged him into the house.

They were slowed down by an

introduction to the half-dozen people who maintained the lodge while it was empty. Apparently it took nearly a hundred when the lodge was full. Selsor never wanted to be anywhere close to the place when it was full; royal hunts sounded terrifying.

Finally, finally they were able to escape, and Jenohn even had the sense to arrange for dinner to be brought to their room, and their luggage left in the hall for the moment.

"They're going to think you brought a strumpet along for a month of rich-people behavior," Selsor said.

Jenohn laughed as he dragged Selsor up a set of stairs and down the hall to a door all the way at the end. "Your jewels are the color of my eyes; I think they know you're a bit more than a strumpet."

"Only a bit more?"

That got him a grin that was almost entirely mischief, but held a surprising hint of shyness. "I admit I was hoping for mostly strumpet."

"You never hope for anything," Selsor replied as he shoved the door open and stepped into an absolutely beautiful room. "You just declare what will be and barrel on until you turn out to be right, one way or another."

He yelped in surprise as he was grabbed and swept up, cradled by Jenohn's arms supporting his ass as he was held aloft, looking down at Jenohn, who grinned up at him. "That's true."

"Put me down, unless your prediction for this weekend was that I'd fall and smash your face. You've already broken your nose twice this month, let's not make it thrice."

Instead of setting him down, Jenohn carried him over to the bed and toppled him down on it, then stepped back and simply stared—rather, *stared,* starting at the bottom and working his way up, eyes hot enough Selsor half-expected to catch on fire. "If you've been wanting to fuck me that bad, why haven't you done it so far?"

Jenohn shrugged one shoulder. "Barreling about getting my way can only go so far, and after hearing all the awful stories of people who tried to use you, with and without your permission, I didn't want to be one more bastard forcing himself upon you."

Selsor laughed, heart giving a happy lurch, spreading warmth through his chest. "Jenohn, you showed up out of nowhere, basically forced me to help you, activated my jewels illegally, declared I belonged to you because I accidentally almost killed you, and dragged me home. If I didn't purposely zap you for any of that, do you really think I'm going to get upset that you finally get around to showing me what you can do in bed? Stop behaving out of character and come here—naked."

He'd been stupid to think Jenohn's eyes

had burned before, because now they were so hot he moaned, which just spurred Jenohn on. He discarded his clothes hastily, then climbed onto the bed and set to work on Selsor's, starting with a searing, claiming kiss that left his lips throbbing, then moving on to kiss and nip and suck every bit of skin laid bare.

By the time Selsor was finally naked, he was trembling, aching, whimpering at every touch and teasing caress. "Are you going to fuck me?" He reached out to fondle the cock that was in proportion with the rest of Jenohn's ridiculous, marvelous mass.

"I just want to hear you scream my name," Jenohn replied. "The rest is details. Though I suspect a good fucking is what you like best."

"There you go being right again," Selsor said. "Get to work."

Jenohn laughed, and moved away briefly to fetch something from one of the tables on either side of the bed. He returned with a porcelain jar, and the scent of jasmine filled the space around them as he opened it.

"So you just keep that in your bedroom here?" Selsor asked.

"No, I do not, so get mad at me," Jenohn said with a grin. "I had them add for me just for this trip. When I'm here working, I'm too busy to have any sort of fun, even if I'd wanted. When I'm here to have fun, it's not this kind of fun. I'm not much for sex with people I don't care about."

Selsor dragged him down and kissed him thoroughly. "Good answer."

"I always have good answers." Jenohn drew back and resumed his delightfully tormenting touches, this time adding in slick, warm fingers pushing and teasing at Selsor's hole.

"What I want to know is if you can deliver a good fuck," Selsor replied.

That earned him the cocky grin that got Jenohn in so much trouble. Selsor loved it more than he would ever admit. "Have I ever failed to give my mage everything he needs and wants?"

"Shut up," Selsor replied, flushing and looking away.

Jenohn just chuckled, and pushed a second finger in alongside the first, curving and crooking his finger with expert skill, leaving Selsor writhing and begging on the sheets.

"Now, damn you," Selsor gasped out, thrusting against his fingers, aching for *more.*

Jenohn gently withdrew his fingers, then spread Selsor's legs further apart and dragged him in close and lined up his cock.

He didn't just shove right in, thankfully. As delightful as that would be, it'd have to wait until Selsor was more used to him.

"Must you be so ridiculously large *everywhere*?" Selsor asked, then moaned as Jenohn pushed in a bit more.

Hot, smug chuckles washed over him, chased by warm lips grazing his throat. "You like my muscles, especially when I come in all sweaty and tanned from the sun."

"I have absolutely no idea what you're talking about," Selsor replied, even as he groaned at the image of a half-naked, sunbaked Jenohn coming in dirty and mussed from playing with what often seemed every child in the city.

Jenohn worked himself in deeper, grinning smugly throughout, hands hot and heavy where they gripped Selsor's thighs. "You know what my favorite sight of you is?"

"Do I care?"

"Yes," Jenohn replied, grin never faltering. "I like when I first wake up, and walk by your room, and you're still asleep. Your hair always comes loose of the braid you put it in, and you're always smiling softly, like you're having a good dream. I'm always torn between going in to kiss you awake, and leaving you to sleep."

Selsor didn't know what to say to that, so he settled on the usual. "Clearly you just settle on leaving me to sleep, like the dunce you are. Now less talking, more fucking me."

Jenohn kissed him, then pushed the rest of the way inside, leaving Selsor moaning and shuddering, stuffed full and aching pleasantly. Then he slowly, gently withdrew, until he was barely still inside, and pushed back in.

Selsor groaned, untangling his fingers from the bedding to grip those enormous shoulders. "More."

Obedient as ever when it came to Selsor, Jenohn set to fucking him in earnest, hips working, muscles bunching and rippling, eyes like blue flames as they watched Selsor. His face went hot, from the exertion and the intense staring, but then Jenohn hit that spot and Selsor howled, head thrown back, digging his nails into Jenohn's shoulders.

Over and over Jenohn drove into him, until his thighs burned and he threatened to overheat, sweat plastered to his skin, making the sheets stick to it, and stinging in his eyes. He didn't even need a hand on his cock, just came as Jenohn drove into him again.

When he could breathe and focus again, it was in time to moan through a last few, overstimulated thrusts before Jenohn buried his face in Selsor's throat and came with a body-racking moan.

After a few minutes, Selsor pushed at him. "Move before you suffocate me, you slab of beef."

"Never had beef," Jenohn said with a chuckle. "Not something we ate growing up, and I always prefer to eat goat or lamb in the palace."

"I prefer fowl, especially duck," Selsor replied, lips twitching at the absurd turn of conversation.

Jenohn rolled off his and sprawled on his stomach on the bed, large and beautiful and utterly perfect, no matter how often Selsor made fun of him or complained. "Was that satisfactory, my mage?"

A reflexive acerbic remark tried to rise up first, but Selsor tamped it down and instead replied, "You always are, my soldier."

Jenohn's smile was like the sun coming out.

Close of Day

THE JEWELS OF BANGKOK

Baxter carefully removed all his jewels for the day, setting them on a velvet salver for staff to take away and store properly. He and Lucid possessed so much stuff—inherited, gifted, bought—that it was all catalogued. He picked out their clothes at the beginning of each week, Lucid chose the jewels, and the servants took care of the rest.

One of the servants came up to help remove his jacket and shirt, both of which had such elaborate fastenings that doing them up himself was just this side of impossible. Across the room, Lucid and Elton were already dressed in lounge wear, though from the way Lucid was sitting, Elton wasn't going to stay in his clothes for long.

That suited Baxter fine.

He thanked the person who'd been helping him and finished undressing himself, then pulled on lounge clothes that were alike in style to

Lucid's, but black instead of gray. When the servant had gone, after pouring Baxter a drink, he picked it up and made his way leisurely across the room to join his lovers.

Because contrary to what the rest of the stars thought, he saw Lucid as his lover more than his brother. They hadn't been raised as siblings, not really. Nothing about their life had ever been typical or average or, arguably, normal. They'd been their mother's ultimate experiment, her greatest success story, and their father's heirs. Though in the eyes of most they were siblings, the legal fact of the matter was that Lucid had been created first, and they'd cloned Baxter from him. Miniscule genetic changes had been made after that, while they sat in incubators growing at a controlled rate, subject to the every whim and desire of their mother—who had loved them, dearly and sincerely, but no one had ever forgotten they were also the pinnacle of a lifetime as one of the greatest geneticists in the IG.

So they'd been raised as companions, in life and in business, more than as brothers. And when the whole world looked at you and saw one where two stood… well, it was easy to turn to the only person in the stars who *saw* you and find love, solace, and acceptance that no one else could provide.

"You look pensive, pretty," Baxter said right before bending to kiss him breathless, enjoying the sweet taste of him, the honesty of his kisses. Right from the start, Elton's lack of artifice had been his greatest draw. Not once in his entire life, until that moment Elton entered it, had they met someone who didn't know who they were, or figure it out almost immediately.

Elton had only been confused, and then angry, and throughout it all he'd been smart, beautiful, and captivating. There were days Baxter still couldn't believe Elton wanted them, this life, which even with all its luxuries could be arduous, thankless, and above all dangerous.

Cheeks flushing as Baxter drew back, Elton licked his lips. "I was, uh, lost in a stupid thought."

"Oh?" Baxter sat next to Lucid on the small sofa right across from Elton's chair, draping an arm across the back of it and leaning in to kiss him. He knew Lucid's mouth as well as his own, knew precisely how he'd slide his lips and move his tongue, how he'd taste at any given hour of the day, exactly how to bite and tease and torment, when to abandon all of that to simply be sweet and soft.

Eventually drawing back, exchanging a brief smile, he turned to an even more flushed Elton and said, "So what was your thought?"

Giving a faint laugh, Elton said, "I was actually wondering when you two, uh… kissed the first time."

Baxter didn't have to look to know the slow, evil grin overtaking Lucid's face. Practically purring, Lucid said, "You want to know when I first fucked my brother, pretty?"

Elton abruptly looked ashamed. "Sorry. You probably get that question all the time. It's none—"

"We don't mind it from you," Baxter said. "No one has ever seen us kiss, let alone fuck, except for you. They don't even know that we do it for sure, though I think it's the favorite fantasy on the 'scape."

Lucid snorted. "I *know* it is; we've sued several companies for defamation. Doesn't really stop them, but the money they have to pay in fines and court costs is more money to dump into charities and such."

Baxter twisted to give Lucid a look. "You never told me we sued people for making tacky porn about us."

"I just assumed you knew," Lucid said, drawing a thumb across Baxter's bottom lip, then pushing it into his mouth, making a soft, approving noise when Baxter obediently sucked it. "Everyone thinks you're the bossy one. I'm not sure why, given they can't even tell us apart."

Drawing away, snickering, Baxter replied, "Because you're *loose*—id, obviously."

That got a fist tangled in the front of his shirt, and then Baxter was dragged to the floor and put on his knees right between Lucid's thighs. "Put your loose lips to work, brat."

Baxter obeyed happily, pulling Lucid's pants down and off, then bracing his hands on those lovely, trim, muscled thighs and swallowing his cock deep. Fingers curled affectionately in his hair, stroking and petting, Lucid happy to enjoy his mouth at leisure while he talked to Elton.

"We were fifteen," Lucid said, breath hitching only the barest bit. "We weren't each other's firsts—mine was a person I met while away at school. Baxter's first fuck was a guest here, some visiting princess from the SE."

Pulling off Lucid's cock, Baxter replied, "She was a countess, not a princess."

"Get back to work," Lucid retorted, and this time used him roughly and quickly, spilling down Baxter's throat in only minutes, then dragging him up to further abuse his mouth, leaving his lips pleasantly sore and throbbing. Then he reached across the way and dragged a hard, flushed Elton into his lap, making quick and easy work of his clothes.

Despite the months they'd been together already, and that they were in their private, highly secure suite, Elton still flushed at being naked in Lucid's lap in the front room. It reminded him of the time he'd been late to a meeting because he'd stopped the lift he and Elton were on to push him up against the one-way glass and fuck him while staring down at people who would gladly kill to be able to see them.

Playing with Elton's cock, nibbling at his throat and jaw, Lucid said, "We were fifteen, in the midst of a party. We'd abandoned it in the aftermath of having someone say to our faces that we should just pick one name, since it was obvious we didn't really need two. I'm sure people had already been saying it for years, but no one had ever said it to us. Father threw them out, and we ran away to our room and wound up fucking."

Baxter gave him a look. "What a summary. I was in tears. You were searching for ways to ruin the man. We didn't even have much fun that time, we were too upset."

Lucid laughed. "Yeah, it's not a very sexy story in the end. We were lonely, and tired of no one but our father—our mother already dead by then—being able to tell us apart, of never seeing Baxter and Lucid, just the Jewels." He made a face. "They started calling us that when we were children—our parents' precious little jewels, their perfect matched set."

Despite the hand on his cock, Elton's kiss was nothing but sweet as he kissed them in turn. "I'm sorry. It sounds like you never got to be children, or anything else for that matter."

"Hard to complain too much when you're some of the wealthiest people in the IG," Lucid said, and there was nothing sweet about his kisses. He shifted Elton to straddle him, then heaved to his feet. Baxter trailed after them, in-lens shimmering as he dealt with locks, lights, and messages, all the other little things that went with ceasing to be the Lords of Bangkok for a few precious hours.

Their room was as warm and inviting as ever, a private nook where no one but the three of them ever went, save for a single trusted servant who tidied up what couldn't be automated. The room was decorated in warm blues, creams, and hints of faded gold, with a perfect three-sixty view of Bangkok that was only possible this high up, secreted away in one reaching claw of Black Dragon Tower.

Lucid settled on his knees in the middle of the enormous bed, Elton in front of him, back to Lucid's chest. He moaned as Lucid fondled and stroked, that wickedly talented mouth trailing his throat. Baxter stroked himself idly as he watched from the foot of the bed, enthralled as ever by how beautiful his lovers looked together.

Elton dragged his eyes open, stared at Baxter flushed, mussed, and utterly drunk on feverish desire. "I need you both. In—" He moaned again as Lucid's fingers worked him. "In me."

Baxter nearly came right then, and at Lucid's silent order fetched the lube from the shelf in the headboard. Crawling onto the bed, he kissed Lucid and then moved around to press up against Elton's front. Cupping Elton's head, he devoured those pretty lips until Elton was feeding him breathy moans and needy whimpers, nails digging into his skin as Elton begged for relief.

He broke away from Baxter to groan, loud and long, as Lucid filled him. Baxter knew the feeling well; there were few things in the world that equaled being fucked by Lucid. He nibbled and licked at Elton's lips until a soft touch from Lucid indicated it was his turn.

They all groaned as Baxter gently pushed into Elton's body, cock sliding right against Lucid's, the fit tight, hot, almost too much. But this, *this* was the best place in the world to be: in their private, secluded corner, Elton between them, filled with them. Him and Lucid together, doing only what they wanted, pleasing their pretty together, the rest of the world far away.

Elton clung tightly, head against Lucid's shoulder, eyes blown with lust whenever he opened them. Baxter fucked him with slow, deep motions, moving effortlessly in time with Lucid, kissing them both, panting heavily, lost in sensation and positively aching to come.

With a soft groan, Elton came, spilling across Baxter's skin, shuddering in their embrace.

"Now, Bax," Lucid said, and as easy as that Baxter came, spilling deep inside Elton, the world fading briefly as his climax consumed it—but he still felt it when Lucid followed him a moment later.

When the world came back to him a moment later, it was to find they'd fallen into a heap across the bed. Baxter pulled gently out, kissing Elton softly, swallowing his whimpers.

Lucid rolled out of bed and fetched cloths to clean them up, and got rid of the blanket they'd ruined, throwing it in a chute down to their private laundry room—since anything washed in even the private hotel laundry rooms stood a good chance of winding up at an illicit auction somewhere.

When they were clean, and food and drinks had arrived via a private lift meant for just that purpose, they settled in bed together to watch vids and talk—and for a few hours, be simply lovers together.

THE TOAD PRINCE

Alton slipped into the ballroom by way of his private entrance, and kept to the edge so he could have a few minutes of peace in which to observe the proceedings. His bodyguards stood nearby, old friends and comrades who'd been overjoyed he was still alive and had volunteered eagerly to resume their duties. It had been humbling, and an overwhelming relief, to know he'd been sincerely missed—mourned.

He was well aware he was arrogant to a fault, comfortable with his power and authority, and many other dubious qualities that too often came with being a sovereign ruler. If that odious bastard Grand Duke had done nothing else right, his little stunt turning Alton into a toad had taught him humility, gratitude.

And even if he had hanged the bastards as promised, he only hated them for killing his family and abusing Wesley and Trina. He would always be secretly grateful for what they'd done to him, because if they hadn't turned him into a toad, he might not have ever noticed the beautiful, earnest and sweet man who'd loved him for no good reason at all, and continued to do so despite all the ways Wesley's life would be easier, calmer, and safer without Alton in it.

Even now, as Wesley danced with Trina, his happiness buzzing through Alton's mind, people watched him. Some had come forward with offers of genuine friendship. Others, Alton had seen to it were warned off. Still others waited and watched, seeing how the new Grand Duke would adjust to his abrupt rise in power, what sort of leader he would prove to be.

A figure broke away from the crowd, smiling his familiar playful, crooked smile as he approached Alton and stood next to him, leaning casually against the wall. "So my absolute favorite rumor is that he's fucking you and Trina, and somehow neither of you is aware of it."

Alton laughed. "Stop listening to rumors, Cadwell, they're bad for you."

"They're my absolute favorite thing," Cadwell replied, grin widening.

Giving him a look, Alton replied, "Lemon creams are my absolute favorite thing, but too many of them and I'd regret my life sorely."

Cadwell scoffed. "Your absolute favorite thing is that pretty little duke in the middle of the dance floor, and I think it would be impossible for you to have too much of that."

Affection and lust curled lazily through Alton as he watched Wesley, who laughed at something Trina said before spinning her in a wide circle. His amusement and joy filtered through the bond, adding to Alton's good mood. There was no better feeling in the world than knowing Wesley was happy. "You do have a point."

"Usually," Cadwell said lightly, his smile softening. "I'm sorry I wasn't here. I should have stayed, for Trina at least."

"I'm honored you were so grief-stricken over my death you fled to the country," Alton said with a smile, elbowing him playfully. "Truly. I know how much you hate country life. That you would rather endure that than live here without me is truly touching."

Cadwell scoffed, looking embarrassed and pleased. "It's good to be back; I really was getting sick of tepid socials and pretending to care about shooting unsuspecting animals."

"Much has changed while I was dead, but I'm glad to see you're much the same."

"I'm much like the tide—always predictable, usually fun, occasionally annoying, and fatal to fools." He winked. "I believe it's almost time for the next dance. May I ask the fair princess?"

"I'm her cousin, not her master. If you want to ask her, then do so. I'll give you a slight edge by getting her current partner out of your way."

Snickering, Cadwell sauntered off, clearing a path for Alton to follow, making it easy to reach the middle of the dance floor.

Alton gave Wesley a bow, adoring as ever the way his freckled cheeks went pink. Through the bond, he could feel happiness, a spike of excitement, and a deep, abiding love. "May I have the next dance, Your Grace?"

"Stop calling me that," Wesley replied, taking the offered hand and going easily as Alton swept him into the dance as the music started. Worry and disbelief filled the bond, along with thoughts of not being good enough, that he might possibly harm people with his inexperience. "I still can't believe you gave me his title."

"It's *your* title." Alton kissed his nose before sending him into a twirl. As they came back together, he added, "He was your father, it was always yours to rightfully inherit, no matter how much of a contemptible ass he was about it. You're much better a grand duke than he could ever have dreamt of being. Now, enough of that, sweet Wes." That got him more flushing, a hint of lust mingled with exasperated fondness. Alton grinned. "I actually had something else I wanted to discuss with you, now that everything has calmed down and you seem to be fitting well into your new role."

Wesley eyed him warily. "I'm starting to get really suspicious whenever you call me 'sweet Wes' in public."

Alton laughed and kissed his nose again, then pulled him a trifle closer than was proper and murmured in his ear, "Believe me, I'd much rather be calling you that in private."

"Behave!" Wesley hissed, but there was no mistaking the look in his eyes, even without the sharp spike of desire in the bond. He was made to be loved, adored, and spoiled rotten, and it was a crime that so few had ever treated Wesley decently, let alone given him all he deserved.

"If I was capable of behaving, I'd never have been turned into a toad in the first place," Alton replied.

Wesley sighed. "I don't understand how you can joke about it."

"Better than letting the more negative effects get to me." Before Wesley could fret, he barreled on, "Stop distracting me. In fact, let's speak somewhere else." He dragged Wesley off the dance floor, ignored everyone trying to get his attention, and finally found a moment of peace and quiet on a small balcony. He yanked the curtain closed so they were slightly closed off from the ballroom.

"Now I'm really worried."

Alton dragged Wesley into his arms and kissed deeply, precisely as he'd been aching to do all day while they were both occupied with other things. It was far too easy to push Wesley up against the wide stone railing and enjoy that sweet, addictive mouth at his leisure. Wesley never did anything with less than his whole heart, and being the focus of that was enough to bring Alton to his knees in all manner of ways.

With an effort, he finally tore himself away. "Let me ask my question."

"You're the one who kissed me," Wesley said with a laugh, fingers stroking and caressing where they were still wound in Alton's thick hair.

"It's my favorite thing to do." He kissed one scarlet cheek, then drew back, reluctantly pulling Wesley's hand from his hair and holding both of them to his chest, stroking the back of them. "It seems silly to me that my royal paramour—"

"That is the most ridiculous way to call me your lover that I have ever heard."

Alton laughed. "That's what they call you. Anyway, it seems silly to me that you're still using that tiny room all the way across the palace. I was hoping you would just move into the chambers next to mine in the royal suite."

"That's for your spouse."

"We'll have that discussion when the mourning period is over," Alton said with a grin, absolutely delighted with the surprise and hope that Wesley couldn't hide. Despite all Alton's instruction, and Wesley's acumen with everything else regarding the bond, he was hopeless at blocking his feelings. It was one of the things Alton loved best about him. "For now, I would like you to live with me. You'd have a bedroom, a salon, and an office all to yourself."

"That's a very… firm step."

"I should hope. I'm quite firm about keeping you—and keeping you close. You are my bonded after all. There's also that tiny detail about being in love with you."

Wesley's eyes took on a sheen, and he ducked his head in a futile attempt to hide his tears.

Alton pulled him into a hug, kissing the top of his head. "Surely you already knew that."

"Yes and no. It's a tad overwhelming to go from loving my idea of a man I thought was dead, to loving the real thing more than I thought was possible, when that man is the king and I was—am—a nobody."

"You're everything," Alton said, and tilted his head up to kiss, mouth fitting to Wesley's like that was its sole purpose in life was to kiss this beautiful man breathless. He let his own love and adoration fill the bond, until Wesley was practically melting against him, eager and pliant.

After a few minutes, Alton drew back slowly, savoring that wickedly addictive mouth. "So will you move into the royal suite with me?"

Shy eagerness trickled through the bond. "It would be nice to be closer to you, possibly see you more often. People will talk even more than they do now, though."

"Let them. It's all envy anyway. They all wish they were me."

Wesley laughed. "I'm pretty sure they all

wish they were me."

"Then they're fools," Alton said, dragging him into another kiss, this one leaving them both panting and unfit to return to the ballroom. "Would you like to see your new rooms now?"

"I'm fairly certain that question is only permitted one answer," Wesley said with a laugh. "Of course I do, as much fun as I have dancing."

Alton kissed him one last time, then led him down the stairs into the garden, where they could easily slip away back to his rooms. The bodyguards would catch up eventually, if they hadn't already predicted where he'd end up.

In Threes

THE WITCH IN THE WOODS

The king was kissing him. *The king* was *kissing him.* Him. The boring, homely witch who'd never have met the king—Thane, his name was Thane and he wanted Anson to use it—if he hadn't invited himself to a three day festival.

Anson's head spun with too many thoughts, too many emotions, all of them demanding attention but only winding up as noise in his head. Normally he quieted the racket by way of work, or doing battle with weeds and thieving rabbits.

Right then, though, he simply threw himself into the kiss, throwing one arm around Thane's neck to hold him close, the other hand braced on a marvelously-muscled arm. He had no idea how long this dream would last, but he intended to get everything out of it that he could.

Eventually, though, Thane drew back, panting against his lips for a moment before withdrawing entirely, stepping back and seeming to gather himself, eyes skimming around the room.

Anson flushed with embarrassment. Normally he didn't care what anyone thought of his little cottage. His parents had built it all on their own, living in a tent for months while building their house stone by stone. It had the main room, which was mostly taken up by his work tables, shelves, and chests, but there was also a little sitting area, a pantry, a cellar, and a bedroom. The whole place smelled of herbs and magic, and every now and then a hint of his mother's honeysuckle perfume, forever captured in the home she'd loved with all her heart and bestowed on her youngest when she'd passed. Anson was proud of it, loved it just as much as his mother had, but next to the palace it must look hopefully shabby and dull.

"You have a beautiful home," Thane said, finally looking at him again. "I'm sure it must get lonely, living out here all on your own, but to me it looks like a nice respite." He smiled, but Anson could see the exhaustion in it, the strain—wondered if Thane was *letting* him see it, which just made his heart trip-trap all over again. "Even when I'm in my chambers, there are bodyguards, servants. Always people. You've no idea how hard it was to come inside by myself. I was only allowed to come at all by bringing four men with me."

"There are people outside?" Anson jerked

forward. "Are they trampling in my garden? They'd better not let the horses—" He broke off at Thane's chuckles, and the warm hands that curled gently around his flailing arms, bringing them to a rest between him and Thane. "Sorry."

Thane scoffed. "No need for that. But I promise my bodyguards are civilized, and former farm boys all. They know their business when it comes to green things." He smiled faintly, a bit impishly. "I'm the only danger to your garden, since I don't know carrots from turnips until they're put on my plate, so I'm the one you need to keep under close supervision."

A laugh burst from Anson, making Thane look pleased and a touch smug. "It's a good thing you're in here with me, then, Majest—Thane."

The mischief faded, leaving only a cautious sort of happiness, hopefulness, as Thane drew him close enough they were sharing breaths again. "I like hearing you say my name." He brushed a soft kiss across Anson's mouth, and Anson would hate how easily it made him shiver except he liked it too much. He liked everything about and involving Thane too much. Him, a nobody little witch in the woods. Besotted with the *king*. This madness was never going to work. Leave it to him to want to go to a fancy party in the hopes of meeting somebody, only for that somebody to be the most out of reach person in the world.

Except he was in reach, very very in reach,

and Anson didn't want to ever let him go.

Thane kissed him like it was his sole purpose in life, which was breathtakingly addictive. Anson wanted to keep him there forever, or maybe drag him into the bedroom, or maybe just down to the floor.

More than anything though, he simply wanted Thane there, with him, in any capacity at all.

How had this happened? He'd created charms of destiny for two spoiled, ungrateful brats, and hoped in return to just dance and talk and pretend he was part of things. But this immediate, utter *rightness* felt like he'd cast three charms, for three brothers, and stumbled his way into the arms of the best one.

Thane drew back, nuzzling his cheek briefly, and said in a delightfully husky tone, "As much as I would love to continue doing this, I did come with a bit more purpose."

"You did?" Anson tore his eyes from Thane's mouth.

That got him a wounded look. "Did you think I only came out here to tumble a witch in secret and then go home?"

"What?" Anson forced his brain to work. "No, that's not what I meant. I mean, you're making it hard to think, move away." He flushed hot at how stupid he must sound.

Thane grinned, but obediently stepped away. "I came to ask if you'd come and spend a few days with me at the palace. A week or so, where we can spend more time together—when I'm not working anyway. I'd understand if you can't though; you must have work of your own, and gardens cannot simply be thrown in luggage."

"I don't live that far outside the city," Anson replied, heart pounding, chest filling with hope and anticipation. "I can always come back here for anything I'm missing. Most of what I work with is dried and such, anyway, and that can be packed."

The way Thane's whole face lit up, with surprise and a boyish happiness he clearly didn't experience often, made Anson's heart hurt. It seemed a crime that this man who stood at the center of everything should know the same loneliness Anson had spent so much of his life feeling, after his parents died and his siblings moved away seeking bigger and brighter things, with only a rare letter sent back to the cottage. Oh, wouldn't he love to see the looks on their faces, when they realized their youngest brother had taken up with the king.

"So you'll come?" Thane asked.

Anson finally offered a smile of his own, letting the same wary happiness on Thane's face overtake him. "I would love to. I am just a witch, though. I don't know anything about your way of life. You may change your mind about taking up with someone who knows more about herbs and magic than people."

"No," Thane said fiercely. "I know almost nothing about magic, but I know it works best and strongest in threes. Three brothers, three destinies, even if that's not what was originally cast or intended. Right?"

"Right," Anson said shakily. "I should have realized it myself, much sooner than I did. Magic has a will of its own. Three brothers, three destinies, three—" He broke off, choking on the words, disbelief clogging his throat and stinging his eyes, the joy was that fragile.

But Thane was there to finish it for him. "Three true loves, just waiting to be realized."

"I'm glad you have more sense than your brothers," Anson replied, "though I do hope they grow up and realize their own happiness."

"Me too, but right now I'm more interested in *our* happiness. Did you want me to help you pack? I can bring my bodyguards in, or send for staff."

Anson twitched at the idea of so many people mucking about with his stuff. "No, but thank you. I'll pack the herbs and such myself." He lifted his head, chin jutting out slightly. "However, you can come and help with my clothes right now, if you wanted."

"It would be my pleasure," Thane replied, making Anson laugh as they tumbled their eager way to the bedroom.

Family Schemes

HOLD STILL

"May I have this dance?"

Esen started, nearly dropping his wine glass, as the familiar voice struck him. He turned, barely noticing as the glass was taken deftly from his fingers, and stared up—and up—at Armia, his former betrothed. "Um."

"Please," Armia said, smiling pleasantly, the kind of smile he'd never given Esen back when they'd been engaged, and extended a hand, which was covered in a beautiful white glove that held the barest rainbow shimmer. He wore a waistcoat that matched them, with breeches and evening jacket of a delicate matte gray trimmed in gleaming silver buttons. His white hair was pulled up into a braid wrapped around his head, with little opals and diamonds scattered throughout it.

Armia was beautiful, like a prince from a wondertale, but they'd always clashed, and Esen had not in good conscious been able to go through with their marriage—even if defying his family had cost him everything.

It had all worked out, as he was currently the lover of the queen's secret bastard son and happier than he had ever been, but it was hard to forget all the pain that had resulted from simply wanting both him and Armia to be happy.

So why in the world was the man who'd always fallen just short of despising him now smiling pleasantly and inviting him to dance?

Curious despite himself, Esen took the offered hand and let Armia lead him to the dance floor. As the strains of a familiar Flower Turn started up, he felt easily into the steps and tipped his head back to stare in open question.

Armia chuckled softly. "I know I'm the last person you want to see—"

"Only because you hate me," Esen said, unable as ever to be anything but honest or silent. It had been one of their biggest reasons for clashing.

"I never hated you," Armia said. "I am deeply sorry I handled our engagement so poorly, treated you so horribly."

"Um—oh." Esen stared. "It's—it's all right. I think the problem was our families, really."

Armia's face soured. "Yes, our families. Which is the reason I sought you out tonight." They parted for a particularly complicated spin, then came back together. "Your family is coming here, because they have caught word that you are paramour to His Grace."

Esen wrinkled his nose. "Why do they care? They disowned me."

"Something they've realized was a mistake, now you are bedding a man vastly more powerful than I could ever be," Armia said dryly.

"Oh." Esen sighed. "They want to use me for their games again."

"Just so, only this time they're going to be far more ruthless about it. His Grace is not a prize they're willing to let go."

Esen didn't laugh, but only because Gaston was slowly teaching him a bit more about containing his thoughts. "I think if they attempt any games with Gaston, they will realize they're not fit to play them."

Armia's brows rose, then he laughed softly. "I see your lover is coaxing out more of your teeth. I'm glad. You'll need them to survive all the court will start sending after you, once they accept how deeply Gaston cares for you—and you for him."

Esen flushed. "I should be used to the fact I'm so obvious by now."

"In a room full of artifice, I am appreciating more and more your honesty is rare and precious," Armia replied. "We would have made terrible spouses, but perhaps we could work on being friends?"

"I would like that," Esen said. "Thank you for the warning regarding my family."

Armia gave a bare nod. "Is there anything I

can do to help?"

"No, I'll attend it. The benefits, I guess, of having a powerful lover." Esen frowned, shoulders drooping slightly. He hadn't gotten involved with Gaston for the money and power, but there was no point in pretending he did not benefit from both those things. As little as possible, but it was impossible to be lover to the much adored secret child of the queen and two powerful chieftans, without finding life significantly improved.

Not that he couldn't stand on his own feet these days. He'd traveled enough with Gaston, and increasingly alone delivering messages for Her Majesty, that he had plenty of income of his own. He was also gaining a reputation as a reliable messenger and guide, which was incredible given he was a Sylph. But it was true that he would never have Gaston's power, and there were more than a few who coveted it.

Including, it would seem, his conniving family. Esen stifled a sigh and smiled at Armia. "I appreciate you coming to warn me, given you had all the reason in the world to leave me to my own devices."

Armia shook his head slightly. "I admire you were willing to say no, while I was just resigned to going along with it for the 'greater good' of our families. I'm sorry your family does not appreciate who and what you are, and instead only rejects you for all that you refuse to be."

The dance came to an end, and they bowed to each other. "If you need help after all, just send word to me. I'm an old hand at scheming family." Armia smiled crookedly, squeezed his hand gently, and vanished into the crowd.

Esen abandoned the ball entirely, and headed for the suite he shared with Gaston. The front room was a delightful clutter of *stuff*: books, fabric swatches, pattern books, mail, lap blankets, cards, games… It was so far removed from the barren life he'd known before Gaston. It was cozy, comforting, vibrant with lives being lived.

He went over to the writing desk and penned a letter to Queen Marga. Normally he would not presume upon her time so, but he refused to let his family hurt Gaston in any way, and Her Majesty would fix the problem before it even became one.

Once he'd sent it off, he sat and fussed with the stack of pattern books his tailors had dropped off that morning, making further notes on the new outfits he'd be ordering, adjustments and tweaks, questions to ask the tailors. The best thing about all his new income was that he could buy all the clothes and jewels and shoes that his heart desired.

If his ridiculous lover didn't try to buy it all for him first, of course.

He'd just switched from patterns to fabric swatches when a knock came at the door. When he opened it, one of the queen's personal footmen stood in the hall. "Her Majesty would like you to come and speak with her further regarding your message."

"I'll come at once." Locking the suite, Esen followed the footman through the halls to the royal wing, and eventually to Her Majesty's favorite sitting room.

But it wasn't just Queen Marga who waited for him. "Gaston!" Esen flew across the room and all but threw himself into Gaston's arms, laughing delightedly when he was swept up and kissed soundly. "You're home early." As the queen laughed, Esen recovered himself, stepping back and straightening his clothes. "It's good to have you home."

Strange, mismatched eyes sparkling, Gaston replied, "The matter wrapped rather abruptly when one of the problems suffered a heart attack. Not my strangest job, but certainly among them. I hear I have arrived just in time to be forced into marriage."

Face burning, Esen said, "I'm sorry. I would have tried to handle them myself, but I'm still utterly hopeless at all the court games, and telling them off directly never does much good."

Marga waved an arm breezily. "They'll be attended to, never fear. It will be a nice change from the law-revising sessions that are dragging on." She sighed. "Four more weeks of arguing Chiefs and councilors, nearly all of whom want the suggested changes but don't like these things cost money."

"You'll get them to come around, Mother. You always do."

She sighed. "I just wish they did not insist on being so difficult about it first. But that's my problem, and right now we need to address your problem." She drummed her fingers on the armrests of her plush, dark blue armchair. "The easiest solutions are to take away their abilities to do anything at all. I will insist they make the disownment final and official. That's step one. Step two…"

"Do not bring up the princess," Gaston said, shooting her a look.

Marga's return look was a cross between a pout and admonishment. "Why ever not?"

"I have a lover, I'm happy as I am, I'm not going to be foisted upon some princess just because you want me to have a title you think is my due."

"It *is* your due," Marga said fiercely, eyes turning shiny, filled with old pain. "You are my son. The son of two chieftans. You should be a prince." She ducked her head. "I still hope there will come a day I can publicly acknowledge you, that all this stupid nonsense will cease and I can be openly proud of my *son* instead of just overly fond of one of my problem solvers."

Gaston crossed the room and pressed a kerchief into her hands before gently embracing her and kissing her cheek. "Mother, we've had this discussion a hundred times. I have no complaints about my life. You threw a duchy at me, I'm wealthy, I worry for nothing except the occasional lousy place to sleep when I'm traveling. I'd rather have parents who love me in secret than openly revile me."

"Yes," Esen interjected quietly. "The former is vastly preferable to the latter."

Gaston sent him a look of apology, and deep, abiding affection, then turned back to Marga. "Please, Mother. There's no reason to drag some poor, unsuspecting princess into this mess. I don't need a wife. I have Esen."

Esen frowned, head tilting. "But then we could be like your parents, right? Isn't that what you've always wanted?"

Gaston flinched, and stepped away from his mother, fussing with his handsome smoke-gray jacket. "What makes you think that? I've never mentioned any such thing." He looked at Esen, remorse and shame in his eyes—and a great deal of worry. "Have I made you feel like you're not enough? Done something? I swear—"

"Oh, mercy, you do take after Gillis, worrying about a hundred problems that don't even exist," Marga said with a fond sigh.

Esen's puzzlement only grew. "You haven't done anything wrong, if that's what you're asking. But I always sort of took it as understood that two would be three eventually. It's the way you talk about your parents, their arrangement... other little things. I'm sorry, I guess I should have said something, instead of assuming, but I thought you, uh, knew I knew."

Gaston stared at him a moment, wide-eyed and slightly panicked at the edges—then deflated with a rueful laugh. "Ever ten steps ahead of everyone, my little Sylph. You have the vision of the sun and the wisdom of mountains." He held out his hands, and when Esen took them, gently reeled him in to kiss his nose. "You would not mind us someday being three, if we found a third who would suit?"

"I think you should meet this princess," Esen said, laughing when Gaston sighed and Marga gave a single, sharp laugh of victory. "If Her Majesty thinks so highly of her, she must at least be worth meeting, right? I think you should be a prince, too, and happy, and maybe she will accomplish both those things."

"What about you? I can't marry two people."

Esen smiled. "I like being just me, in that way. My family never saw me as anything but a stepping stone to power, someone to be sold off for the wealth and glory they wanted, without ever caring what I wanted for myself. It's fun being your… what's the word… paramour. That's the one. I'm the Duke's eccentric, scandalous paramour. Refused a good marriage, just danced with the man I rejected, drowning in pretty clothes and jewels that my lover buys to keep me appeased and…" Esen frowned. "What's the other word they used."

"Biddable," Margo said sweetly. "They think you're a little brat who is made biddable with expensive things."

Gaston rolled his eyes. "For crying out loud."

Esen laughed. "They're not wrong that I like expensive things."

"Which you buy yourself and refuse to let me buy once in a while."

"I was picking out my new winter wardrobe when I was summoned."

"Of course you were." Gaston kissed his nose again, then his mouth. "You really don't mind my mother's scheming?"

"Why would I? I'm enjoying being the scandalous lover; you would make a fine prince; and you've always wanted to be three like your parents." He clapped his hands together. "Just think of the rumors when I remain your lover after your marriage."

"You're becoming something of a brat," Gaston said, and just like the way he said 'little Sylph' he turned the word into something precious, instead of the insult Esen had heard all his life.

"So…" Marga prodded gently, though she rested with her chin in one hand, smiling fondly as she watched them.

Gaston heaved a long, dramatic sigh and

raked his hands through his hair. "Fine. I will meet this princess. But I promise nothing more than that."

"Finally!" Marga said, throwing her hands into the air in victory. "Your fathers will be delighted. We're all going to do dinner, and tell you all about her. Go get changed, and come to the gold dining room in two hours."

"Yes, Your Majesty," Gaston drawled, and then Marga was gone, leaving them alone in her salon. He pulled Esen back into his arms, and this time kissed without restraint.

Esen wrapped his arms around Gaston's neck and kissed him ardently back, with every bit of the longing he'd felt while they were apart, all the adoration and affection he had for this man who loved him as he was. Didn't consider him a freak or weirdo. Didn't think him a failure, or completely useless. Simply loved him, indulged him, and above all grounded him. He was more appealing, more enthralling, than even a cool spring wind filled with the scent of new greens and budding flowers, and sweet sunshine after a long, bitter winter.

"You really don't mind all this princess nonsense?"

"I seem to recall that once upon a time, there was a discussion about threesomes, and some naïve young man asking how three people can have sex. You've yet to demonstrate that to me. I'm rather hoping this will work in my scandalous favor."

Gaston laughed so hard his head wound up resting on Esen's shoulder for balance. "You! It's a good thing you're not good at court games, because I fear for the whole of the court." He cupped Esen's face and gave him another toe-tingling kiss, the kind that left Esen aching and longing, then withdrew. "Come on, we'd best go get ready for dinner. If we're late, my mother will never let me hear the end of it."

Esen pouted. "Do we really only have time to get dressed?"

"Depends on how quick you can be," Gaston said with a slow grin and a wink. "Shall we find out?"

Gloating

THE ROSE AND THE FOX

Briar enjoyed the salty sea air, the cool breeze it wafted over his face, a pleasant contrast with the searing sun beating down on him. The ocean was not as beautiful as the Laughing Forest, the enormous lake with its trio of crashing waterfalls and clear, cool waters, but it was certainly a fierce beauty all its own.

Unfortunately, that beauty was besmirched by the cluster of people surrounding Reynard and flirting shamelessly with him. Once upon a time, such a thing would have infuriated him, sent him storming off convinced that he'd been a fool yet again in the matter of love.

But the handsome man with auburn hair and forest-green eyes tinged with faerie magic belonged to him, true love's kiss and all.

Catching Reynard's eye, Briar crooked his head in a silent request for his presence. Without hesitation, Reynard excused himself and pushed through the crowd, making straight for him. Briar smirked and rose from where he'd been leaning against the stone wall that separated the beach from the town. "Having fun, Fox?"

"Who wouldn't, in such a beautiful place?"

Briar lifted one shoulder. "Traveling is interesting, but I'll always love our forest best."

Reynard carded his fingers through Briar's hair, then gently pulled him into a soft, lingering kiss that silenced all the furtive whispering—most of them questioning Briar's parentage and occupation—from the group that had been flirting with Reynard.

Drawing back with a smile, Reynard twined a lock of Briar's hair around one finger. "Your skin is turning gold, my love. Looks good that way."

"Another few minutes it will go from gold to red," Briar grumbled, but with a smile. "I could do with some cool shade and something refreshing to drink."

"Then it shall be done." Reynard offered his arm, and Briar took it—and gleefully threw the smuggest smirk he knew, the kind of smirk that only came with being a spoiled, royal brat, over his shoulder. The little group seethed at his gloating, and he was not above admitting he enjoyed every moment of it.

"What has you looking so smug?" Reynard asked as they sat at a table in front of a cheerful, brightly decorated tavern that had only just enough walls to keep it standing, and was otherwise open to the sea and sun, with charming, gigantic parasols to protect each table and its diners from the scorching sun.

Once they'd ordered their drinks and something to nibble on, Briar said, "I was making it painfully clear to your little would-be suitors that their cause was a lost one."

Reynard grinned, happy with a touch of disbelieving bashfulness. "I rather like belonging to a possessive prince."

Briar tossed his hair, chin jutting out. "Good, because I put up with a lot of nonsense before I could finally have you."

"Yes, the succumbing to a curse was a bit much."

"Oh, please, you're going to gloat about being the one to break it for the rest of our lives—and probably our afterlives."

Reynard's grin softened to a smile full of so much warmth and affection that it almost hurt to look at. All for him. Briar might bluster and fuss, but he could not imagine going another day of his life without that smile, this man, a part of it. "Of course I'm going to gloat forever. Until nothing remains of us but stardust. I'm the Fox of the Laughing Forest, and I stole the heart of the beautiful, untouchable Prince Briar."

"Oh, shut up," Briar said, cheeks warming, and sipped his sangria.

Reynard just chuckled and sipped at his own drink, flirting idly with the server who brought their food a few minutes later, but his eyes always just for Briar.

Nibbling at a piece of cheese, Briar said, "Have you heard from your merry band recently?"

"I got a note this morning. They've invited us to join them at a place a few days from here, in time for a summer festival that apparently involves a great deal of drinking and lewd behavior."

Briar lifted his eyes to the sky. "I am not engaging in public acts of lewdness with you. I may no longer still be crown prince, but I am still *a* prince and if word got back home about me behaving the perfect wanton at some festival—"

"Oh, come now, you could be a little naughty." Reynard batted his eyes playfully, then gave him a perfect, pleading pout.

Briar sighed and said nothing, but the grin Reynard didn't bother to hide said they both knew he'd won.

Not as though it was a hardship. Briar's only other real lover had been a cowardly bastard who'd denied their affair when Briar had needed him most. He would gladly revel in the attentions—sweet, lewd, and otherwise—of this man who never stopped happily bragging about Briar to anyone who made the mistake of holding still long enough.

He reached across the table, offering a hand, and smiled as Reynard immediately tangled their fingers together, and lifted them to kiss the back of Briar's hand. His eyes gleamed with fairy magic, and for a moment, the salty air seemed to carry a hint of pine and roses. "Shall we see what else the day has in store for us, my love?"

"I think if we go back to our room, you'll find out what I have in store for you," Briar replied.

Reynard grinned his fox smile, and dropped coins on the table before dragging him away.

The Healer's Spouse

BRIGHTLEAF

Thorley looked up from his soup and beer as familiar words washed over him. Pixie tincture. Blue willow. Ogre grass. Two of those were used to treat a variety of maladies. One of them was not. He looked around for the source, and found it at a nearby table, where a child sat cradled in the arms of a tired-looking woman, an equally worn man next to her.

But the words were actually coming from a cretin with carefully tousled hair and a smile so greasy it could be used for cooking.

"He'll be just fine in a couple of days," the greasy man finished, presenting a dark, cheap glass bottle stoppered with candle wax and twine.

Thorley stifled a sigh, because he knew exactly how this was going to go, but he had to try anyway. "No, he won't."

Three heads turned to look at him, eyes going wide as they registered the goblin who'd been in their midst the whole time. The greasy man sneered at him. "What did you say, goblin?"

"I said, that won't cure his fever, or whatever is causing the fever. There's no such thing as pixie tincture. Ogre grass can be used to help with pain, but it has to be combined with certain other things, like brightleaf or sweet ivy. Blue willow is great for fevers, but it has to be used in moderation, especially if given to a child, and should be cut with mint and moon rose. Whatever potion you're selling them, it'll probably make the child feel better just long enough for you to get out of town."

The man puffed up like a pissed off earth wyrm. "What would a nasty *goblin* know about healing? I'm surprised they even let your kind into this respectable tavern." Next to him, the family looked scared and confused, and were being careful now not to look at him.

Thorley sighed, gathered up the goods he'd spent the day trading for, and laid coins on the table for his meal, as this was actually one of the few places that didn't charge him double up front and bring him the charred leavings at the bottom of the pot and beer that was mostly water. "I don't want any trouble. I was just trying to help. When that stupid potion invariably fails, there's a healer about two hours from here who will be more than happy to help, and he'll do it for free." He rose, and all three at the table reared back, huddling inward as they registered his full height, all his earrings glinting in the firelight. He stared at the greasy little charlatan. "How much for that stupid tincture of yours?"

"Ten bits."

"You really are a thieving ass," Thorley said, and dropped a whole silver on the table. "Ask the tavern owner to break it for you, see they get their twenty bits in change. If not, I'm good at finding greasy little monsters in need of slaying. Understand me?" He bared his teeth.

"Get out of here, you nasty little goblin," the man said, a tremble in every word.

Thorley left, lifting a hand in farewell to the tavern owner, whom he'd once saved when the tavern caught fire. Thorley had later found the bastards who'd tried to burn it down, and seen to it they paid in full and then some.

He whistled all the way home, and smiled as he was greeted by the sight of a familiar figure washing off by the rain barrel, half-naked and gleaming with water in the light of the lamp he'd brought outside with him.

"Not that I'm complaining," Thorley said, "but why are you outside bathing at this hour?" He glanced up at the moon. "It's near to midnight." He set the bags of goods by the door to deal with in the morning, as none of it required immediate attention.

"A few children in the next village came down with a bad case of gremlin pox. I have the tonic done, but it took hours and faerie moss combined with elf weed and weeping daisies makes for a sticky, sickly-sweet mess no matter how careful you are." Geoffrey finished toweling off, then threw his arms around Thorley's neck and drew him into a sound, lingering kiss. "You're home early, keeper. Didn't trust me to go unsupervised another day longer?"

Thorley laughed, lightly dragging his sharp claws up and down Geoffrey's back, enjoying the delicate shivers that resulted. "Ran into an oily little pixie tincture seller, tried to talk sense into the family he was swindling. They didn't listen, and tried to make me leave. Decided it was better if I just came home."

"I see," Geoffrey replied with a sigh. "I'm sorry." He kissed Thorley again, tongue flicking playfully against his sharp teeth. "Come inside and I'll make it all better."

Growling, Thorley swept Geoffrey up in his arms and carried him into the house, smiling at the delighted laughter that resulted. All these years later, he still was in awe that this sweet, earnest, handsome healer who deserved the world had settled for a grouchy half-goblin with more kills to his names than relationships.

He laid Geoffrey down in their bed, then went to take care of the lamps. When the house was closed up and dark, save for a single lamp on the wall above the head of the bed, he stripped off his clothes and crawled into the blankets, where he was greeted by a warm mouth and eager hands.

There was no better homecoming than this: wrapped in Geoffrey's arms, sliding into his welcoming heat, swallowing every gasp and moan, the way Geoffrey said his name as he trembled and came. Falling asleep to soft, panting breaths, wrapped in warmth, the smell of sex mingling with the perpetual scent of plants and herbs, Geoffrey's head on his chest.

~~*

Two days later, Thorley was outside preparing some of the mutton Geoffrey had traded for tinctures. He was going to smoke most of it and store it for winter. The remaining he already had slow cooking in the oven out back to eat that night.

He'd just finished covering everything in the spice rub and putting it in a tub to rest for a bit when the sound of people coming up the path drew his attention. He went to the bucket of water he'd drawn earlier and cleaned his hands, then moved to preparing the branches he'd cut earlier for the smoking. Good evergreen, with fruit rinds thrown in to add flavor and sweetness.

The visitors came around the corner as he was still kneeling there, and he wasn't remotely surprised to see a familiar couple, the man carrying the sick child in his arms.

"Is this it?" the woman asked, sounding near to tears.

Thorley rose slowly, so they could see him past the table where he'd been working. "If you're looking for the healer, yes, this is the place."

They stopped short, gasping audibly and rather dramatically, as they recognized him. "You're the goblin from the tavern," the woman said, bottom lip trembling, eyes taking on a wet gleam. "Are you the healer?"

"No," Thorley said. "He's inside. Come on, he'll be more than happy to help." He motioned for them to follow.

They hesitated, shared a look, then the woman set her shoulders and headed toward him, and they followed Thorley into the house.

"Done already?" Geoffrey asked, looking up from where he was working on patching up some of their clothes. "Oh, we have company." His smile turned into a frown as he registered their faces, and the child cuddled against the father's chest. Putting his sewing aside, he pushed to his feet and bustled over to them. "Do you know what's wrong with him? Here, put him on the bench there." He motioned to a large, wide, padded bench in his work area, where he often had people sit or lay while he helped them.

The mother wiped tears from her face. "No. He's had a bad fever for two weeks now, can barely keep down food and water, and only small amounts at a time. He just sleeps all the time, moaning about aches and pains. We've tried everything." She started crying. "Your friend there tried to warn us about the man who sold us a tonic, but we didn't listen, and I'm worried now that we've only made it worse."

"Most pixie tinctures are little more than feverfews and mild pain killers, cheap stuff anyone can find in a field and stuff into a bottle of watered-down alcohol," Geoffrey replied. "You said two weeks. What was he doing around the time it struck?"

"Just playing in the fields behind the house like he's done a hundred times," the father said. "I searched the whole thing several times, trying to find something that might have bitten or stung him, but I found nothing. Can't find a mark on him anywhere, and by now it'd be healed up anyway."

Geoffrey's lips pursed in thought. "There's a few things it could be. Let's get his fever down first. Thorley will fix you both some tea, while I make a different tea for your son. My name is Geoffrey, this is my husband."

"Husband?" the woman stared a moment, then shook herself. "I'm Anna, this is my husband Benjamin and our son Marcus. Thank you for helping us. The other healers just gave us some manner of feverfew tea and sent us on our way."

"I'm sorry you were treated so poorly," Geoffrey said.

Thorley smiled faintly in fond memory as he went to make tea, the good, strong dark tea, with plenty of honey and cream. He brought it to them with bread, some of the pears they'd traded for that morning, and some cheese. "Eat. Rest. Your son will be all right."

"Thank you," the woman said, looking at him, then looking away, cheeks flushing. "I'm sorry we were so rude to you before. You were trying to help, and even if you weren't, there was no call for rudeness when you'd done nothing wrong. We didn't even notice you until you spoke."

"You were worried about your child," Thorley said, shrugging one shoulder. His mouth quirked. "And to be fair, nobody expects a goblin to prattle on about herbs and tonics."

Anna smiled faintly. "It's true that's not usually what they talk about. But I am sorry. We saw you were a goblin and made assumptions, and still you paid for the medicine and ensured we had plenty of money to spare. You're exceedingly kind."

"I'm married to a healer; it sort of rubs off. We met because my brother got hurt and was dying, and Geoffrey was the only one who'd help us. If not for him, my brother would be dead. Instead, he's married to the local Marquis and I got to keep the healer." He winked. "Drink up before it gets cold. I'll be outside if you need anything."

On the other side of the room, Geoffrey was already lost to his work, bustling and muttering to himself, the pungent scent of blue willow filling the air.

Checking the meat, satisfied with how it looked, Thorley got it strung up on poles and then racked up for smoking. Once the smoke was going, and he could trust it to be left unattended for a few minutes, he went inside to see how matters progressed and if Geoffrey needed anything.

He found the parents crying, and the child sitting up, slowly sipping at a cup of tea that Geoffrey held for him. "Good," Geoffrey said, smiling in that way of his that could melt the stoniest heart. "Just a few more sips, there you go."

"He already looks better," Anna said. "How did you do it?"

As Marcus finished the tea, Geoffrey ruffled his hair and stood, returning to his work area. "I think your son was probably bitten by an ogre fly. It's a mild bite, most people don't even feel it, and at worst they feel an itch. Then the spot will ache and itch for a few hours, maybe leave a small bruise for a couple of days. But some people, like your son, react badly to the bite. In adults, it's just a bad fever and some mild aches for a couple of days. But he's young, so he reacted far worse. But the blue willow is helping the fever, and I added a couple of other things to help with the aches. Another hour or so, he should be up to eating properly, and with a couple of days of good rest, he'll be back on his feet like nothing ever happened."

Anna burst into tears and buried her face in her hands. Benjamin cuddled her close, burying his head in her hair to hide his own tears.

Thorley fixed them more tea, and got a porridge started for Marcus that should be ready by the time he felt like eating. He added sugar, cinnamon, and plenty of dried fruit that would fill out and soften as it cooked.

Leaving it to simmer, he returned to his smoking, pleased to see it was coming along.

Trading, smoking, and cooking weren't the most exciting activities in the world. Most would call them mundane and boring, even tedious and annoying. But Thorley would gladly take on the most boring chore in the world over having to return to a life of traveling around killing things just to earn enough money for a meal and relatively clean bed. The chores meant he had a home to take care of, a life to maintain. The kind of life he'd never really had, with a mother who couldn't bear to look at him, parents who were secretly glad to finally see him leave.

Anyone who looked down on a secure, peaceful life was a damned fool who didn't deserve it.

When the meat was done smoking, Thorley made certain the fire was well and truly out, then took the cured meat to the shed behind the house, storing it with all the other preserved foods he'd been steadily working on, and barrels and chests of various dried goods. They'd want for nothing when winter hit—and he hadn't even started on the fruit yet. That was tomorrow's project, while Geoffrey turned the rest of it into jams and wine.

Carrying in a few things for dinner, he set them on the kitchen table and then went to clean up—in the creek, rather than simply at the rain barrel, since he doubted their guests wanted to see a naked goblin wandering around.

Returning to the house, he was met by Geoffrey pressing a finger to his lips, followed by a nod toward the living room. Thorley's mouth curved as he saw Anna and Benjamin fast asleep on the sofa. Nearby on the bench, Marcus had fallen asleep in the middle of eating his porridge.

Geoffrey helped him get dinner going, and once the soup was bubbling away, drew him into a soft, lingering kiss. "I like having you around, goblin."

"That's good; otherwise this wedding ring would be a bit awkward," Thorley replied, and grinned as Geoffrey used his chest to muffle his laughter. Kissing the top of his head, Thorley then went to make up the guest bed while Geoffrey kept an eye on dinner and the sleeping family.

Letting Go

THE TROLL

Giles wiped his brow, then set a new log on the stump and swung the axe, splitting it deftly in two. He'd started at dawn, when the air was still so chilly his breaths misted, gulping down a hasty cup of tea before setting to work. The sun was well up now, and he was near to half done.

All in all, a pretty good start to the day.

He paused to catch his breath, and looked toward the house—just as the door opened, and a handsome figure came out carrying a steaming tray. Though Kenzie had been with them for just over six months now, the excitement and cautious happiness never faded.

Kenzie smiled as he reached Giles, and set the tray on a table Giles had improvised from some old cords not worth chopping up for burning, and some leftover plank scraps from the shed they'd built to house all of Kenzie's herbs and other healing supplies and tools.

Of which there was a shocking amount.

Giles had never realized that healing entailed so much. Kenzie always smelled faintly of herbs and flowers, and he was forever collecting, drying, bottling, powdering, pickling… and so many other things. It had taken them most of the past six months simply to build the shed, acquire all the implements and tools to fill it, and then all the herbs, flowers, mushrooms, and more.

The twins loved helping Kenzie almost as much as they loved Kenzie himself. From the moment they'd woken up and met him, and learned he used to be the troll, he'd been their favorite person in the world. Giles might be jealous if he didn't find it absolutely adorable. If he didn't love how seamlessly Kenzie fit into their life, like there'd been a spot there the whole time just waiting for him to show up.

He set the ax in the stump he used for chopping, and gratefully took the mug of tea Kenzie offered. Like everything else, the tea had vastly improved since Kenzie's arrival. It was never burnt or stale, always fragrant, perfectly steeped, flavored with all manner of things—including honey, which Kenzie seemed to have a knack for acquiring. "Thank you."

Kenzie leaned down to kiss him, tasting of tea and honey himself. "Least I can do for the man who never seems to stop working, he's so determined to take care of us all."

Giles laughed. "Says the man who has an entire apothecary behind the house. I've been to the village healer multiple times, and I vow she doesn't have even a tenth of all that you've acquired since leaving the bridge. And you're always fussing about what's still missing."

"I was trained by one of the best healers in the kingdom, before I went gallivanting off with a lover who was quick to abandon me," Kenzie replied, and reached out to tuck back an errant strand of hair that had escaped the tail Giles had bound it in. "I kept up with my studies by way of books, and learning from healers in the camp and all the villages we traveled through. I used to have my own books, journals filled with all my notes and recipes. Who knows where they've ended up now; hopefully in the hands of someone who can use them."

"Should we trade for something like that?" Giles asked. "Books? Journals? I suppose we'd need the ink and all, too." He gnawed thoughtfully on his bottom lip.

"Stop your plotting. I don't need any such thing," Kenzie replied, and kissed him again. "I was merely explaining why I know so much. I had the luxury of a fine teacher, and after him many other teachers, because I traveled. Mistress Constance is a perfectly fine healer."

Giles wasn't convinced of that, but his opinion was soured by the fact that she treated Giles much like everyone else—as though he'd committed some crime by daring to be born to parents who flouted rules and had no time for closed minds. "You're not that much older than me, but you've done so much," he said wistfully.

Kenzie kissed him again, drew him in close and held him, despite the fact that the after chopping wood for a couple of hours Giles was hardly pleasant to be around. "I've got a good six years on you, silly, that's not nothing. If you want to pack up and travel and see the kingdom, we certainly can."

"No, gods no, not with the twins. Can you imagine? We'd kill them or they'd kill us or—" Giles shuddered thinking about all the trouble they could get into with a whole kingdom to play in. It was hard enough keeping them out of trouble when they only had the house and fields. "Maybe once they're all grown up and off terrorizing other people."

Snickering, Kenzie kissed him again then stepped back and tugged him over to the improvised table. "Eat. I know you must be hungry, given how late you worked yesterday, your further exertions last night..." he winked. "And the work you've already done this morning."

Giles flushed. Finding time to themselves could be a tricky thing, but mercy when they managed to get it... Brent had always been eager to get off and scared of getting caught with the son of the village disgrace. Those harried fumblings had always left Giles feeling disappointed and ashamed, but he'd done it again and again hoping that something, anything, would change.

Kenzie was nothing at all like Brent. He was eager, enthusiastic, cared enough not to rush selfishly to the bit that most interested him, in fact seemed to take the most pleasure in Giles' pleasure. And he knew so very much more than Brent and Giles had ever figured out together.

"Go away before I try to do something we'll certainly get caught at," Giles said, and shoved Kenzie away when he grinned evilly.

When Kenzie had gone, with a last parting leer over his shoulder, Giles set to eating. Kenzie had made bread the previous day, taking it out of the ovens—another project of his that had taken them days, but been oh so worth it—right as the sun was setting. It was slathered with butter they'd traded for, and more of the honey Kenzie had collected.

So many little ways that life had vastly improved since Kenzie had arrived. Someone to help him, someone who loved him, loved the twins. Who knew so much and seemed happy with their quiet, simple little life, even though it was clear he'd lived a vastly more colorful one once.

Finishing the bread, and the slices of apple alongside it, Giles went back to work chopping wood. Once he was done with this, he'd clean up and put on fresh clothes, then go out to check the traps. Hopefully there'd be some good hares in them. Then he needed to repair the baskets so they'd have them tomorrow to haul the laundry to the creek, since laundry for four people was an all-day endeavor, especially with the twins.

And somewhere in there would be lunch, and playing with the twins, and maybe a few stolen kisses in the shed.

He finished with the wood, then headed off to the creak with the bundle of clean clothes he'd brought along and got washed off.

When he returned to the house, however, it was to find the twins in a tizzy. "Visitor! Visitor, Guy! Someone's come to see us."

"Stay in the house," Giles said. "Where's Kenzie?"

"Out front," Heath said, pouting. "He said to stay inside, too."

Giles laughed and ruffled their heads, then went to see what was happening.

He found Kenzie, a cart, and three men in front of his house, with a fourth, prone figure in the back of the cart. "What's all this?"

"Something wrong with Brent," one of the men said, and Giles realized it was his little brother, barely fourteen years old now, and he seemed close to tears. "We was working, and then all of a sudden he said 'ouch' and fell over. Hasn't woken up since, and Mistress Constance couldn't figure it out. She tried some things, but they only seemed to make everything worse."

"Let's get him inside," Kenzie said. The men hefted, and they got him into the house and settled on a cot that Giles dragged out of the corner to be closer to the low-burning fire that was going.

Then he went to fix food and drink for the scared group while Kenzie got to work.

He found Brent's brother, Callen, outside trying not to cry. "Here, have some cider. You look like you could use it."

Callen sniffled and took the mug Giles held out. "Thank you for helping. I know Brent doesn't deserve it, not after the way he's always treated you. I'm sorry to just barge in like this. We just didn't have nowhere else to go."

"Bad history doesn't mean I should leave him to die," Giles replied. "He wasn't the one who threw the dagger."

"That was Wake," Callen said darkly. "No one is best pleased with him. Ain't okay to go 'round killing people, and nobody wants that kind of trouble." He looked at Giles, then down at his mug. "I'm sorry everyone is so mean to you. I never understood it."

Something unknotted in Giles chest, and he managed a genuine smile as he gripped Callen's shoulder. "It's okay. People are set in their ways, and don't always react well when that's disrupted. I'm glad you're not like the rest of them. Gives me hope for Heath and Hadley."

Callen looked to where Heath and Hadley were playing at the far edge of the field, right at the edge of the woods. Giles wanted to call them back, because they knew they weren't supposed to go that close, but he left it for now. "They seem like really cute kids."

"They always like to make new friends," Giles said. "If you want to keep an eye on them for me, I'd be grateful, since Kenzie will probably need my help here shortly, and I've still got chores to get done."

Brightening, Callen said, "I can certainly watch them—and help with chores, too. Least we can do since you're helping with Brent. Just let me know!" Then he was gone, bolting across the field to the twins, who immediately stopped playing and drew together to inspect the new arrival.

Giles left them to it, silently wishing Callen luck, because he had no idea what he was in for.

Back inside the cabin, Kenzie was bent over Brent, but it wasn't hard to tell the hovering presence of the other three men was making him tense, especially as they wouldn't stop peppering him with questions.

"Let him work," Giles said gently. "Best thing you can do. If you want to keep occupied, I've got a trap line that needs to be checked on, and there's always wood that needs chopping."

Relief flooded their faces at the offer of having something to do, and before Giles could even tell them where to go for the traps, they were out the door and gone. Shaking his head, amused despite himself, Giles looked to Kenzie. "Need anything from me?"

Kenzie looked at him with affection and gratitude. "You just took care of it."

"Know what's wrong?" Giles asked, going over to the little stove in the corner of the cabin that served as the kitchen and pouring a mug of tea. He took it over to Kenzie, who kissed him in thanks.

"It's definitely a spider bite," Kenzie said. "The strange thing is that I think it came from a spider that shouldn't even be around these parts. But one of Brent's friends said his mother had some fancy lumber brought in for the new furniture they're building. Spider could have stowed away on that. Hopefully it came alone, and not with a breeding partner or children." He sighed. "Would you keep an eye on him? I've got him stabilized, but I need to go prepare the antidote. Come for me if he takes a turn for the worse."

Giles nodded, kissed him, then pulled up a chair and sat beside Brent, occasionally changing out the cloth of cool water on his head that was helping with the fever.

The last time they'd spoken had been when Brent and the others had tried to cross Kenzie's bridge. Giles would never be entirely fond of Brent, not after years of hoping Brent would see him as more than a hasty, illicit fuck only to be treated horribly time and again… but without Brent's bratty behavior, he might never have broken Kenzie's spell, so he was willing to let bygone's be bygones.

"Do you miss him?"

Giles startled, and looked up, staring at Kenzie's downcast eyes and frown. "Miss who? Oh, I'm an idiot. You mean Brent. What is there to miss?"

"You were staring at him so pensively."

"I was thinking he was a bastard to me for years, but I'd let it go because it was that bastard behavior that led to me accidentally stepping onto your bridge. I don't like him, but I can't hate a man who led me to my true love, even if he did it accidentally." Giles laughed.

Kenzie broke into one of his absolutely beautiful smiles, and kissed him briefly before sitting opposite him and setting to work on Brent. With Giles's help, he got Brent sitting up enough to get him to swallow a cup of something that smelled like bad perfume and probably tasted worse. Kenzie's concoctions rarely tasted good, but they always worked.

By the time he'd finished that and gone on to treating the wound itself, which had left Brent's right leg swollen to nearly twice its size around the bite area, the others had come in from helping him out with the chores.

"How is he?" Callen asked.

"Fine," Kenzie said. "He'll probably wake up in another hour or so. Stay for lunch, and you can take him home by the time you're done. Just mind he stays off the leg for the rest of the week, and drinks all of the tonic I'll send home with you."

"I will!" Callen said, and hugged Kenzie tight. "Thank you! Especially since I know you've every reason to hate him."

"I'm a healer," Kenzie said gruffly. "My duty is to help everyone who needs it—everyone. Now come on, I'll make the tonic and show you how it's done in case that spider shows up again."

Giles lifted a hand to signal he'd get started on lunch, and let the remaining men cart him off to see the hares they'd collected from the traps, and all the other work they'd done for him.

Men who'd barely talked to him before, and had been part of the ruckus at the bridge.

Life was strange, but at least of late it seemed to be the good kind of strange.

Visitors

BLACK MAGIC

Koray would never get used to the way people insisted on helping him with things like bathing and dressing. He could do both those things perfectly fine just by himself—especially now his hair was not as long as it used to be, thanks to children and foolish pranks.

But he admitted, on days like this, when he was already exhausted and the day wasn't even half over, and this was the third time he'd had to return to his room to change, that the help was appreciated.

He set aside the work robes he'd been in, and let Mela and Russ, his personal servants, help him into the formal court robes. The runes embroidered along the edges shone in the sunlight spilling through the windows. The tapestries that usually covered them were gone entirely, so someone must have taken them for their monthly cleaning.

Mela smoothed down the hood of his over

robe so that it lay neatly against his back, then brushed and braided his hair, arranging it so the braid wound around his head almost like a crown, an impression furthered by the jeweled black and purple roses she tucked into it.

On his fingers were several rings, another ridiculousness he could not become accustomed to. One was his wedding ring, a simple gold band with Sorin's name carved inside. Another, on his right pinky, was his royal signet. Yet another was set with a pentacle made of onyx and amethyst that marked him as the High Necromancer. Still others were gifts, talismans of protection and power given to him by Neikirk, and a beautiful antiqued silver ring set with a dark, gleaming ruby that had come from the North, a gift from Brekk.

"Thank you." The servants bowed and bustled off to tidy away his other clothes and such, and Koray headed off to the main hall.

The assembly was still standing, awaiting the arrival of the Court of Five. Koray's arrival made four, and he wasn't surprised that Sorin was the only one missing. Sorin and Cerant were probably the busiest of the five of them, given their roles, but Sorin's role often demanded he go far afield and so he had the hardest time getting back for matters like this.

This matter being the arrival of delegates from a country that Koray had never even heard of before Neikirk began tutoring him in the evenings on all the things he'd never had the opportunity to learn growing up. He hated he'd never be as educated as the others, who all knew multiple languages and where to find any given country on a map and the history of those countries, and so many more things. Koray and Brekk always stood apart in that.

But they had their own strengths, though it had taken him time to truly appreciate that.

Koray took his seat. They were arrayed across the dais, a row of five, the tops of the high backs marked with their respective crests so all comers knew who held which role: High Alchemist Neikirk; High Priest Cerant; High Paladin Sorin; High Necromancer Koray; and High Warlock Brekk. The Court of Five, designated by the Goddess herself, so never again did the people have to worry about one single monarch controlling everything.

Sorin arrived a few minutes later, casting them all an apologetic look as he took his seat. Though none of them had more rank over the others, it was true that Sorin and Certain were regarded as the 'rulers' more than the rest of them in the day to day of things. Koray and the others tended to work more in the shadows, or alongside them, doing all the little things those two didn't have time for, or which was best suited to their respective offices.

Once he was settled, and assured the others were ready, Sorin bid the guards to admit their guests. Normally such things were handled by the Grand Steward, but this particular group was making a huge fuss and demanding a proper audience, and as they'd all actually been on the premises that day, or near enough in Sorin's case, they'd decided to grant it.

Their visitors walked in pompously, reminding Koray viscerally of every noble who'd ever shoved him into the mud, or set servants to beating him and driving him away. Every person who'd denied him food or a place in the stables just to be warm and dry for a night.

They wore beautiful, if strange, clothes, tight fitting and dyed in bright colors and flashy patterns.

The bond he shared with the others conveyed they were equally unimpressed, and Brekk and Sorin were also worried this would erupt into a fight. Something about the visitors made them think soldier, or mercenary, or something along those lines.

Koray was vastly more intrigued by the woman and child at the back of the group, the way the Goddess gently nudged him to them. Unlike the others, the four pompous men who acted like the castle belonged to them, the woman and child walked quietly, heads bowed, mostly hidden by soft veils. They also wore more subdued colors, with only a hint of a simple geometric pattern in their underrobes.

Vastly more intriguing, the child felt like a

necromancer—rather, like they *should* be a necromancer.

"You've insisted on taking our valuable time," Sorin said to the group. "You'd best make it worthwhile. Why did you insist on this audience?"

The man who seemed to be the leader of the group, dressed more floridly and richly than the others, feathers bobbing in his peculiar hat, swept an ostentation bow. In slow, clumsy Vindeian he said, "My king was most insistent we see for ourselves the notorious Witch Court of Vindeia."

Cerant laughed. "Witch court? We aren't witches. I've yet to hear any names, sir."

"Of course, my pardon. I am Lord Bartley Ondole, Duke of Vaar, High Steward of Cormontaine, Voice of His Most Holy Majesty King Wesix."

Sorin quirked one brow. "That's a lot of words to simply say you're the royal spokesman and envoy of a nosy king. What do you lot really want? I sincerely doubt you traveled thousands of miles simply to gawk at us. Cormontaine is well-known for its magic; there should be nothing remarkable about ours."

Ondole introduced the rest of his party, save the woman and child, who it seemed may as well not be there. Why? Koray held off asking for the moment, but his curiosity and the Goddess's interest burned distractingly.

He watched them surreptitiously, especially the way the child whispered to the woman, almost as though they were translating for her.

"It's not every day that a king is deposed and replaced by a group of five witches."

Cerant's mouth flattened. "We are not witches."

The man gave him a look so patronizing, Koray was amazed Sorin didn't rise up and knock it from his face. "You use magic that is unique and rare, and that the general populace could never hope to access. That is the very definition of a witch."

"Maybe where you come from," Cerant said coldly, causing the man to recoil. "Here, that word is a slur, an outdated term for anyone blessed with the goddess's power, before it was understood to be a gift from Her. We are not a court of witches, we are the Court of Five, the five points of Her star, ordained by Her to care for Her people and land, and right the wrongs committed by our ancestors, and the mistakes we ourselves have made."

One of the other men laughed, a cold, derisive, even mean sound. "You're in charge because you think a goddess appointed you?"

"Did you not call your own king holy? Is he not also ordained by the Goddess to protect and care for your people?"

They all looked at each other, having some

silent conversation, and finally Ondole said, "His bloodline was long ago blessed by the gods, yes. But only crazy people hear 'voices' of the divine. That sort of witchery is the work of charlatans and the insane."

"No!" the child burst out, dissolving into tears. "I'm not crazy! I'm not!"

The woman immediately tried to comfort her, and looked at Ondole, saying something—but whatever it was, it did no good, because Ondole strode over and backhanded her.

Everyone in attendance roared in outrage, and it was only the guards who managed to keep people back, along with Cerant's clear, deep voice ringing out and demanding silence.

Koray stood and strode down the steps to the dais, and swept up the child—a little girl—as she ran straight to him. Holding her close, he looked coldly at the men who were staring aghast. "Why did you strike her? Why are you treating this woman and child so appallingly?" He motioned to the woman, who after a moment of hesitation, slowly went over to stand beside him, whispering a soft, "Thank you" in Vindeian.

Shifting the girl to one hip, though she was old enough it was heavy and awkward to do so, Koray reached out and took the woman's hand, holding it firmly. Jerking his chin at a nearby footman, he said, "I want the woman and girl moved to their own room, and guards stationed at all times. Have anyone who tries to interfere detained."

"Yes, Your Highness." The footman darted off, and the little girl held Koray even tighter as she whispered what he'd said to the woman, who in turn started quietly crying, squeezing his hand in clear gratitude.

Leaving the rest of the mess to the others, he took them away, leading them to his own chambers and getting them settled with tea and food in the front room.

"What are your names?" Koray asked. "I'm Koray; you may call me that."

"Koray," the little girl repeated. "My name is Lisetta. This is my sister, Rosa."

"Sister?" But as they both removed their veils, he saw indeed the woman was not as old as he'd first thought—late teens, maybe, instead of in her twenties.

They were both lovely, with light brown skin and long, straight, ink-black hair, and freckles across their noses and cheeks. They almost could have been twins, were they closer in age. The only difference between them was that Rosa had green eyes, and Lisette brown. Koray had every faith they would eventually be violet.

"Half-sister," Lisetta said. "We have the same mother. She's married to Lord Ondole. When he was ordered to come, I begged to be allowed to come too. I *had* to come."

"I see," Koray replied, holding back his opinions on a mere girl being married so soon, and to a bastard like Ondole. "How does a little thing like you come to speak Vindeian?"

"She told me to learn it. The voice." Lisetta reached out and picked up one of the little fruit cakes Cook had sent along, a popular treat with all the children in the castle. "Can I have this?"

"Eat whatever you want." Koray nudged the trays of food closer, and poured tea for both of them, making certain to add plenty of cream to the wooden children's cup so it wouldn't be too hot. "The Goddess speaks to you?"

Lisetta nodded, but didn't speak, far more interested in eating the fruit pie as quickly as possible. Koray's stomach hurt, and his heart ached, for he'd eaten like that himself once. Years, now, but at times it seemed only a matter of days.

Next to Lisetta, stroking her hair fondly, Rosa looked ready to cry. Koray motioned for her to eat as well, as he mulled over the fact that the Goddess had brought this slip of a girl all the way across the world to him. Well, both of them, because he did not think Rosa was here by chance either. No, both girls were meant to be here.

The door opened, and Cerant stepped inside, smiling in greeting and murmuring to the girls in their own language. Whatever he said, Rosa burst into tears finally, curling in on herself in the kind of relief that Koray knew all too well. It was *I've really escaped* relief. *Everything will actually be okay* relief.

He remembered the feeling every time

Sorin held him.

"What did you tell them?" he asked as Cerant sat next to him on the sofa, across from the one the girls sat on.

"That they've been granted sanctuary here, and the rest of their party is being put on a ship tonight, and are not permitted back in the country. I don't know what their true purpose here was, and I doubt we ever will, but She said these two were meant to be here. That's all that matters to me."

Koray nodded, and poured them all more tea. "The younger one is a necromancer."

"I think the other might be destined for Sorin," Cerant said thoughtfully. "That is what She seems to be telling me." He spoke to Rosa in her language, and whatever he said, it caused Rosa's face to light up like the sun coming out after a storm.

While they talked, Koray chatted with Lisetta, quietly encouraging both of them to eat all the while.

They were both struggling to stay awake by the time Sorin appeared, blowing into the room like a spring wind the way he always did. "Are they all right?"

"Better than they've been in ages, I'd say," Cerant said, smiling softly as the girls finally succumbed to sleep, curled together on the couch. "The older one is meant to be a paladin."

Sorin nodded. "I've already arranged her

training. I assume you've got priests or courtiers who can help with the language barrier?'

"We'll have them sounding like they were born here before the year is out," Cerant said. "I arranged it before I came here. But we'll let them get settled a bit before we set tutors upon them. Is their room ready?"

"Yes, and guards enough have volunteered to watch their door that shifts are covered for the next twenty years," Sorin said. "If anyone tries to touch them again, they're going to find themselves set upon by the entire castle. Come on, let's get them to their new room." He picked up Rosa, holding her as though she weighed little more than a feather, but as if she was spun from glass.

Cerant picked up Lisetta, and Koray followed them through the halls to their new room.

Once they were settled, with two guards posted at the door and a woman inside to help them once they woke, Cerant headed off back to his cathedral and Koray walked with Sorin back to their chambers. "Not what I expected of the day."

"Nor I, but if we ever anticipated Her scheming, we'd be bored out of our minds," Sorin said with a smile, rubbing absently at his chest where he'd no doubt been playfully jabbed for the jest. He held out his hands, and when Koray placed his own in them, rubbed the backs of them with his thumbs. "I suppose fatherhood was the only thing left for you to conquer."

"Fatherhood?" Koray asked, voice going high—but even as he said it, he felt Her satisfaction in his head. "I don't know anything about being a father!"

Sorin laughed, and let go of his hands to cup his face and draw him into a soft kiss. "Nobody ever does. You didn't know anything about being a leader, and look at you now: the most beloved of us all."

"That's not true by half."

"Shut up," Sorin replied cheerfully. Then his smile turned positively evil. "You also didn't know anything about being a lover, but last night you certainly had no problems—"

"Finish that sentence and last night will never be repeated," Koray hissed, face flushing even after all these years.

Sorin laughed delightedly and drew him into a kiss, holding him close and filling him with all that lovely warmth. He nuzzled Koray before drawing back enough to speak. "Shall we go deal with the clamoring masses, and explain our new children to them?"

"If we must," Koray said, but was smiling as he took Sorin's hand and headed off to explain their new family to the castle.

A Warm Welcome

THREE GOATS

Cornelius laughed as he sat down with his just-made cup of tea and saw that both Billie and Matt had fallen asleep in the middle of eating their pie. He clucked his tongue. "Silly goats."

"Sounds like they had a long day," Robbie said, and set aside his own empty plate to pick up Billie, slinging him over one shoulder and then climbing the ladder to the loft. When he came back down, he nudged Matt, who sleepily heaved to his feet and shuffled off to the loft himself.

Robbie, predictably, finished off their half-eaten slices of pie before clearing away all the dishes to be taken out and washed in the morning and ensured the house was locked up tight for the night.

Then he strode right over to Cornelius, took away his tea, pulled him out of his big cozy chair, and stole the seat, dragging Cornelius down into his lap. "I've missed this—you—so much."

"I don't recall this ever being a thing," Cornelius said dryly, but went easily when Robbie pulled him into a kiss that tasted of apples and cinnamon and home.

Robbie nuzzled his cheek as they drew apart. "Always wanted to do it, sit right here like this with you. Never worked up the nerve."

Cornelius gave into the urge to drape his arms around Robbie's neck and leaned into him, more delighted with this new arrangement than he would ever, ever admit. "Learned some boldness in the city, did we?" he asked teasingly. "Pretty boys and girls teach you a few things?"

"Yeah, that city folk are loud, demanding, and rude." Robbie stroked and caressed him, so much like he had every time they'd cuddled beneath an apple tree and exchanged kisses. "I had a few offers, especially a couple of interesting ones from some fancies. But I told every last one I had a sweetheart back home, and he was a forest lord, and they couldn't compare."

"You did not," Cornelius said, face flushing, warmth filling him that had nothing to do with the fire and everything to do with the silly goat boy holding him. "I'm not a forest lord."

"Forest lord enough, and definitely my sweetheart." Robbie tilted his head up and kissed him again. "Though I admit I thought I'd have to work harder to get back into your good graces."

Cornelius squashed his nerves like he would an insect invading his stores, and murmured in Robbie's ear, "You'd better work hard. The children are asleep, it's been three years, and I'm tired of only having my hands."

"You're an evil brat," Robbie said breathlessly, though there was no mistaking the sudden interest that Cornelius was sitting on. "Want to finish your tea?"

"I don't care about the stupid tea." Cornelius kissed, hard and messy and eager, suddenly desperate now that he'd finally voiced what they'd been dancing around since the other two had fallen asleep.

Robbie heaved to his feet, still holding fast to Cornelius, who clung for dear life, and headed off toward the bedroom. Cornelius called out the words that activated the spell for putting out the fire, and for lighting the lamps in the bedroom. Being a half-human wood sprite who studied magic had its benefits.

"Mercy. You couldn't manage that before."

"I worked hard to get all these fine new muscles," Robbie said smugly. "Couldn't come home all soft and useless, could I?" Once in the bedroom, he set Cornelius on his feet and kissed him, cupping his head and feasting on his mouth like it was a second dessert.

Cornelius keened and clung tightly, still unable to believe that Robbie was home, had willingly come home, had kept his promise. He pushed, breaking the kiss but sending Robbie toppling onto the bed, and made short work of his own clothes. Robbie's eyes widened, trousers tenting obscenely. "Cornelius..."

"You've got a lot of time to make up for," Cornelius replied, and knelt to remove Robbie's socks and tug at the ties of his trousers. He pulled them down, intending to pull them off, but was distracted completely by the bared cock, hard and red and wet-tipped. He swallowed, tried to tamp down on the resurgence of nerves.

They'd only been together once like this, before Robbie had left, and they hadn't really done much that time, both too eager and unsure. But Cornelius had done a great deal of reading in the past three years, and he was determined.

Robbie chuckled softly, and carded a hand through his hair. "I can't tell if you're scared or delighted. But if it's the first, get up here so I can do some of the things I've been thinking about."

"I'm right where I want to be," Cornelius replied, and with a deep breath braced his hands on Robbie's thighs and slowly swallowed his cock. He couldn't go far, and Robbie stretched his mouth nearly to the point of pain, but the way Robbie moaned his name, the way the fingers in his hair tightened briefly, almost pulling, made it all worthwhile.

Cornelius pushed up on his knees a little more, took him a little deeper, sucked a little harder, using his right hand to stroke and tease what his mouth couldn't cover.

He probably wasn't very good at it, but Robbie seemed pleased, to judge by the moans and cries, the way he thrust into Cornelius's mouth when he forgot himself. Cornelius flushed, pleased and excited that he must be doing *something* right. He really wanted to see if he could get Robbie to come, as last time they'd wound up just thrusting messily against each other.

Then Robbie abruptly pulled out, pulled away,

and Cornelius rose, backing away in mortification, face still hot but no longer from excitement. "Sorry. What did I do wrong—"

Robbie surged up, dragged him, and kissed him so thoroughly that Cornelius swore his lips were left tingling. "Wrong?" He laughed. "If that was wrong, I'll never survive you doing it right."

"Why did you stop it then?"

Dragging him over to the bed, Robbie lay him down on it, pushed his legs apart, and settled between them. "Because I really, really want to fuck you, and I'm not sure I have the energy to get hard twice right now. Not after traveling all day."

"Oh," Cornelius said, worries dissipating. He licked his lips and said, "I, uh, have something for that. I bought it from Master Vincent. Just for me, I mean. Not anyone else."

"I wouldn't have blamed you if there had been someone else, you know. I half-expected to come home to find you'd found someone who had the sense not to leave you in the first place."

"Shut up, you stupid goat," Cornelius said, dragging him down into a ravenous kiss that he hoped made clear he had no interest in anyone else. Just his sweet, earnest apple thief who'd come home to him as promised. "Let's see what you can do, Mr. I'm a Fancy City Boy Now."

"I am not." Robbie bit at his lips, then his jaw, then worked his way lower, pinning Cornelius's hands down when he tried to push him away because it was all delightfully too much. "Nuh-uh. I thought about this all the time while I was away. Sitting by the fire. Helping you pick apples. Dragging you into a proper bed and seeing if I could get you to scream."

"You get me to scream, you get to explain to your brothers why."

Robbie laughed. "Like they don't know what I do with the Troll Lord when they're asleep or not around. We raise goats, Cornelius. We learn pretty quickly what's what."

Cornelius's face burned. "Stop talking and do *what's what* before I toss you out of this bed, Robbie Gruff."

That got him an absolutely marvelous grin, hot and shiver-inducing. Then the brat put his mouth right back to leisurely work, tasting, kissing, and occasionally nipping at what seemed to be every stitch of Cornelius's skin. "You—" He gasped and writhed. "You weren't like this when you left, I swear. Not a complaint, mind."

Robbie gave a torturous lick to his cock, then drew back to rest on his heels. "I rented a room in this massive house that was mostly full of... well, prostitutes. They were happy to tell me things, explain as much as they could. They offered demonstrations, but I turned that down."

"You—" Cornelius laughed. "Of all the places in the city, and you asked them those kinds of questions!"

Robbie leaned down to kiss him, bracing himself to hover over Cornelius. "Course I did. Had amends to make, didn't I? Now stop distracting me." He kissed Cornelius's nose, then his mouth, and then pushed away to fetch the oil from the basket that Cornelius pointed him to.

Then he settled between Cornelius's legs again, as easily as if he was meant to be there, or had been there a hundred times already. The first was definitely true, and the second wouldn't take long to make true.

Slicking his fingers, Robbie gently pushed one inside. Too gently. Cornelius groaned and rolled his hips to take it deeper. "More. I can fit three of my own in there, you know."

Robbie's groaned drowned out his, and he gripped the base of his cock with his free hand. "Don't say stuff like that or this is all gonna end too soon."

"Already taking too long you ask me," Cornelius replied, and laughed when that got him a playful swat on the thigh. "Maybe I should—" He broke off with a cry as Robbie shoved two fingers inside him and twisted them just so.

"Better?" Robbie asked smugly.

Cornelius just moaned some more and tried to get *more.*

Thankfully, Robbie was happy to provide, stretching and tormenting and hitting that spot over and over, until Cornelius was sweaty and trembling and *aching*. "Now, you damn goat, before you're left to fend for yourself."

Grinning that delightful wolfish grin again, Robbie withdrew his fingers, lined up his cock, and gently but swiftly pushed inside. He groaned, muffling the noise in the hollow of Cornelius's throat, kissing and nuzzling as he slowly began to move, withdrawing slightly and thrusting back in.

Cornelius clung to his sweaty back, panting against his shoulder as he met every thrust, took him as deep as he could manage, riding the high of being so thoroughly fucked by this man he'd been certain would never come back to him. Because who would choose a half-sprite apple farmer in a dead-end little village when there was a whole city to choose from?

Robbie would, and had, and Cornelius wanted to stay right there like that forever, savoring the lust, the love, the need, the simply happiness of finally being back together.

One more hard thrust was all it took to send him over the edge, and he mostly muffled his shout in Robbie's shoulder, shuddering through his climax and holding on tightly as Robbie thrust into him a few more times and came, moaning his name against his skin.

Cornelius's eyes stung briefly as he simply lay there, calming down and cooling off, holding Robbie close all the while.

Eventually Robbie rolled off him, though he stayed close, pulling Cornelius right up against that broad chest and nuzzling his hair. "So am I back in your good graces?"

"I don't know," Cornelius replied with a smile. "Somebody promised presents and then never—"

"Your present!" Robbie bolted from the bed like he'd just been told a stable was on fire, leaving Cornelius staring after him. He returned after a few minutes, and hastened back into the bed, with such ease that one might have thought it had been their bed longer than a few minutes.

Would he move to their house? Would the Gruffs move to his? Was he getting ahead of himself?

"Here," Robbie said, thrusting a box into his hands.

It was made of gleaming wood, with rounded corners, and a stamp burned into the top, a crest Cornelius didn't recognize. He flipped the little catch and lifted the top—and stared.

It was a necklace. No, a locket. It was silver, etched on the front with two tiny apples. He picked it up gingerly and held it up to let the light catch it—and saw there was writing on the back. *My Home.*

Cornelius lowered the necklace as his eyes blurred. "You jerk."

Robbie chuckled and took the necklace from his slack fingers, and affixed it around his neck, where it fell to nestle in his collar bone. "Sorry you hate it."

Wiping his eyes, Cornelius then dragged him down into a kiss that he hoped conveyed just how much he hated it. "You were supposed to be paying off debts, not buying me silly things."

"I could do both. I never once faltered on the debts; I just earned extra wherever I could so I didn't come home entirely empty handed. Wait until you see the other presents, and all the money I managed to save. We shouldn't have any trouble for a long time, if we're smart and careful."

Cornelius curled his fingers around the necklace, already excited for the morning, when he could cut a lock of Robbie's hair to keep in it. "I don't need presents, or money. Just you, Robbie Gruff."

"You've got me," Robbie replied. "I'm home, that's where I'm going to stay. Though I hope you don't mind you're going to be stuck with a whole lot of goats around, since I'm pretty sure you wouldn't enjoy us moving to your place. The goats like it better here anyway."

"I'm used to goats." He pushed Robbie into the bedding and peppered him with kisses, like he had so many times after they'd spent their day apart and only met up as dark was falling. "Welcome home."

Family Reunion

THE SOLDIER

"Captain."

Grigori turned around from the rack of swords he was going over with his second-in-command, a smart, handsome woman who was more than happy to knock heads around if that's what it took to keep rowdy soldiers in line. He stared at the anxious-looking servant waiting for his attention. "What is it?"

"There is someone here to see you; he says he is your brother?"

A cold knot formed in Grigori's stomach. Emil was here? To see him? "I'll come see him."

"Yes, Captain. He awaits you in the yellow parlor."

"Thank you."

Leaving Zlata to continue working on inventory, Grigori tidied up his already perfect clothes, ran a hand through his hair, and with a long sigh went to see why in the world his brother—the brother who hated him, despised him so much he'd ordered him whipped 300 times—wanted to speak with him.

His back was turned when Grigori stepped into the room. Emil had always been big—of build, of presence, of ideas, of ego. He towered over everyone, beckoning them to him on purpose and unwittingly.

Instead of the uniform he'd been wearing when last Grigori had seen him, however, he was dressed in the more familiar homespun clothes they'd both grown up in. So he must have returned to their parents' farm. How strange to see his brother, the powerful, soldierly figure he'd admired for so long until finding out he went around pretending he had no family, returned to their humble roots, while Grigori stood in palace finery.

He cleared his throat, and Emil turned, emotions flickering over his face before he settled into the carefully trained composure of a soldier. "Grigori. Or would you prefer Captain?"

"My name is fine; you're my brother, after all."

"Yes," Emil said slowly. "I am."

Grigori stepped further into the room and closed the door. "What do you want, Emil? I can't think you *want* to see me, given the last words you said to me."

Emil winced. "I was stupid, and wrong. I was never going to let anyone whip you, Grisha—Grigori. I'd already ordered the punishment reduced to latrine duty for a month, and I wasn't even going to make you do that."

"That's not the point," Grigori replied, though it was good to hear that for all his stupid posturing, Emil hadn't actually ever intended to hurt him. "Why did you insist on convincing everyone you were an only child?"

Thunderclouds filled Emil's face. "Because for once in my damned life, I wanted people to see *me* and not my oh-so-perfect little brother, smarter and stronger and better looking—better everything—than me. You came along and Father and Mama may as well have forgotten I existed, and everyone else followed in their footsteps. In the army I was *me.*"

Grigori stared at him, mouth agape. "Emil… why didn't you just *talk* to me. I didn't know you saw it that way, that you felt—were—treated so. I looked up to you. Just wanted my big brother to think something of me that was positive." He sighed and went to sit down, motioning for Emil to do the same. "You should have talked to me."

"I am trying now," Emil said as he took the nearby seat, a small table between them. "I should have done so sooner, but since being released from duty and returning to the farm, I have been busy with a great many problems. That is one of the reasons I've come to see you." He grimaced. "It's not the reason I wanted to come, please understand. But we've been left with no choice."

"Tell me," Grigori said, frowning.

Emil spread his hands. "There is someone stealing from our winter stores—personal, as well as the village stores to which we all contribute. We have asked the nearby city garrison for help many times, but they never come. I have even gone to see them a few times, and still no one ever comes, and in the meantime the village's winter stores continue to be taken, to the point we will not have nearly enough to get us through. I did not want to come bothering you, especially with our history—my mistakes—but I was left with no choice."

"I will take care of it. The problem never should have been allowed to fester so long, I'm sorry."

Shoulders slumping as the tension left them, Emil said gruffly, "Thank you. That is all I wanted. I will cease to bother you now. I'm certain there is much else you should be doing."

"I'm not so busy and mighty I cannot spend some time with my own brother," Grigori said. "Would you like to stay for dinner? Perhaps meet Vasili?"

"Meet the king who fired me for being mean to you?" Emil asked dryly. "I don't think that's a good idea, Grisha."

Grigori smiled briefly. "It will be fine—though at that, I'm surprised you've never met him before, given you were one of his generals."

"I was always on the front. I met the Steward, I do not recall his name, but never His Majesty."

"Stay, then. Please."

Emil hesitated, then nodded slowly. "If you wish, then, though I did not bring clothes suitable for dining with the king."

"We'll work something out. It was just going to be the two of us tonight, anyway." He rose and motioned for Emil to follow him, but paused as they reached the door. "It hasn't been publicly announced yet, but you should know that Vasili has asked me to marry him."

Emil's eyes widened. "I see. You have managed to do quite well for yourself, Grisha." His mouth quirked. "I was determined to be Commander of the whole army, and now I am back to being a farmer, and my little brother who never wanted any glory at all will be Prince Consort."

Grigori laughed, still awkward and shy about the whole matter. "I'm not used to it yet, not really. I doubt I ever will be. But come, I'll show you around and introduce you to people, and we'll get all prepared for dinner." He smiled hesitantly. "It's good to see, brother."

"And you," Emil said quietly as they headed off through the palace.

~~*

Much later, when the day was done and they were finally alone for a few hours, Grigori sighed. "What did you think?" He started removing his clothes and jewelry, setting the clothes neatly aside for the servants—he'd learned quickly to leave that to them, or earn their wrath for putting thing away the wrong way or in the wrong place—and tucked the jewels away in his case.

"I think farming suits your brother far better than general," Vasili said, taking his hands and drawing him into a kiss. "I think being my captain, and my future consort, suits you. Funny how that worked out."

"Emil said something similar," Grigori replied.

Vasili chuckled. "Things get mixed up sometimes, but fate always sorts everything out to its liking." He lifted Grigori's right hand to his lips and kissed the knuckles. "I hope you are happy with the sorting." He lifted his free hand to rest it against the side of Grigori's face.

Grigori leaned into the touch, eyes falling shut. "If I wasn't happy with where I was, I never would have agreed to make my life a thousand times more complicated."

"Given the way you didn't give me an answer for ages—"

Laughing, Grigori opened his eyes. "It was ten minutes at best, and only because I couldn't believe what I'd just been asked. I still can't believe it." He turned to kiss Vasili's palm "I should run away from the army more often."

"Once was enough I think," Vasili replied with a laugh of his own, as he set to work on Grigori's remaining clothes, casting them aside with a good deal less care. "Now come to bed, before someone comes to me about the west wing being on fire or something.

"If you insist."

Vasili smiled in that delightfully wicked way of his, a smile that no one but Grigori ever saw, much like no one else had ever really seen the man lost in the woods, the man who'd taken a harsh reprimand from a runaway soldier and rather than get angry, had only been miserable about letting him down.

Dragging him into bed, Vasili doused the lights

and pulled the bed curtains, trapping them in a gauzy world all their own. Clever, knowing hands soon had Grigori moaning and pleading, and it took entirely too long for Vasili to slide into him and fuck him until he screamed.

Several minutes later, when they'd gotten their breath back, Vasili kissed the back of his neck, always a prelude to some serious question or discussion. "What do you think of giving your brother a title? Put him in charge of the whole area, instead of just informally taking care of his village?"

Grigori turned. "You'd do that?"

"He's going to be my brother-in-law," Vasili said, and Grigori could feel the smile pressed against his skin. "I do not want him powerless and unprotected, and he's shown he can learn and grow. There's an earldom in that area that's gone unused for decades; I think it might be time to dust it off."

Grigori turned so he could kiss Vasili properly. "You're still the kindest man I've ever known."

"Ridiculous," Vasili said. "You did not know me before I got myself lost in the forest and had to be saved by a man with a truly kind heart. You improve everyone around you, my Grisha. We all would do anything simply for one of your smiles."

"Now who's being ridiculous?" Grigori muttered, pushing Vasili down into the bedding to give Vasili much, much more than a smile.

A Forgotten Face
OF LAST RESORT

Raffé threw a last few bodies on the pile, nodded to the priests and paladins who would be handling the burning, and went to find a bit of wall to prop up. He needed blood and rest, but right then all he really wanted was to hold still for a few minutes. Thankfully, the paladins had matters well in hand and could manage without their commander for a bit.

He really wanted to strangle the damned fool who'd allowed so many dead-walkers to pour into the city, but he'd been one of the first killed. That was usually the case with such fools: they caused needless death and destruction, and escaped facing justice, either by suicide or killed by their own rampant stupidity.

Closing his eyes, he listened acutely to the noise around him, alert to any troublesome sound or shift in the air. Thankfully, he heard only the usual noise that came with the aftermath of battle, as a city came slowly back to life to care for their dead and fallen. He counted thirteen bells, from priests ringing them at the places where people could bring their dead, to be hauled off to temple for proper rites.

A nearby man had twenty-seven silvers in his purse, and thirteen gold tucked into a secret pocket of his jacket.

Seventeen dogs milled about, and one hundred and seven horses were still in the vicinity.

He could smell four hundred and eighty-seven dead; five hundred and thirteen wounded. Seven of those would probably not survive the night.

Seventy-four—

"Raffé?"

Raffé's eyes snapped open at the sound of an unknown voice speaking to him with such familiarity. He stared at the man standing a few paces away, but nothing about him stirred Raffé's thoughts. He was handsome, in a generic sort of way, with chalky white skin, brown hair and trim beard, the healthy build of a man who could afford to put good food on his table and worked hard to do it. He had gray eyes, like the slush that filled the streets when snow started to melt. "Who are you, to speak to me with such familiarity?"

The man's face flushed, and something like shame, humiliation, filled his features briefly. "I beg your pardon, Your Highness. I should not have presumed familiarity, or assumed you would remember me. It has been a few years. But we've heard much about you here, all of it praise, and I was startled to see you in person again and realize that every word was true."

Raffé pushed to his feet, resting one hand lightly

on the hilt of his sword, which marked him Commander-in-Waiting, though really he was more Acting Commander with Telmé's guidance and support. "I am sorry that you know me, but I do not recall you. When and where did we meet?"

The man gave a soft, sad huff of laughter. "We were betrothed, once."

Raffé stared, memories flooding of a life he'd all but forgotten. After a moment, he managed to dredge up a name. "Almor?"

Almor smiled crookedly. "Just so, Your Highness. I should say thank you, for saving us today. I don't know how the dead-walkers managed to breach the city defenses, but I'm grateful the Legion was near to hand."

"We're always honored to serve our people," Raffé replied, still stunned that this was Almor. That he'd so completely forgotten about the man he'd nearly married. The man who'd hurt him, left him alone with his fear and loneliness, on what Raffé had been certain were the final hours of his life. "Are you and yours all right?"

"Yes, Highness, thanks to you and the rest of the Legion. They came close to breaching our home, but didn't quite make it." Almor hesitated, then took a step closer, still stiff and deferential in his demeanor. "I wanted to say I'm sorry, Your Highness, for the way I treated you back then. I know it little matters now, but I owe you an apology all the same and I give it."

Raffé tilted his head to the side, staring pensively. "Why did you turn me down that night?

Simply to satisfy my curiosity."

"Because you'd made it rather apparent that you had more mettle than any of us had bothered to notice," Almor replied. "I thought I was marrying a timid clerk who would do as told and stay out of my way. But you were far, far more than that, or could be, and I suddenly was forced to admit I could not measure up. So like a coward I fled."

"I see." Raffé drew a breath and let it out slowly on a sigh. "Well, it was years ago, as you said, and in the end no lasting harm was done. Indeed, if you hadn't rejected me that night, I might never have gotten to know the man who is now my husband." He lifted his hand to display the wedding mark on the back of it. "We're also going soon to the Reach of the South to consider one of the Grand Duchess's daughters as a marriage candidate." Raffé was both nervous and excited about it, that the new addition meant Alrin would father children. But after all he and Alrin had been through together, it would be strange to see how their dynamic shifted with a third added.

"The legless woman?" Almor asked, eyes widening.

Raffé bristled. "She has a name."

Almor winced and lifted his hands in apology. "Yes, that was crass of me. I am sorry. I was surprised, but that's not an excuse for being ill-mannered. You might be marrying Lady Zoja?"

"Time will tell," Raffé replied. "How are your wives?"

Sadness filled Almor's face briefly. "Tomislava

passed away from illness two years ago."

"Goddesses grant her peace."

"Thank you. I married another woman last year, and she's just borne twin sons this month."

Raffé smiled, truly happy. "Congratulations, and Goddesses bless them with long and fulfilling lives."

Almor beamed, but then turned faintly sheepish. "Bojana is quite devoted to Guldbrandsen and the Legion, as we all should be, and was quite insistent on the names of our new sons. In two more months, at the naming ceremony, they will be blessed as Waldemar and Raffé."

"They—truly?" Raffé stared as Almor laughed. People were naming children after him? "Well I apologize to your child that he is already cursed with that legacy."

"I think he'll learn quickly it's an honor," Almor said quietly, that crooked smile returning. "You would have been a fine addition to our house and home, Your Highness, though I was too foolish to see it at the time. However, you also would have been quite wasted on us, not that you need me to tell you that. I'm glad to see you doing well, and right where you truly belong."

Raffé smiled faintly. "Thank you. And you've leave to use my name, Lord Almor."

Almor's face lit up. "I'm honored. If you've time, you should stop by my house to meet my family. Bojana would be beside herself to have the namesake of one of her children in our home. It would be a blessing from the Goddesses."

"Well, it's not every day a demon is declared a blessing," Raffé said with a laugh. "I must return to my duties, but leave me your address and I will try to stop by before I depart."

Almor did so, and ran off smiling, clearly in a rush to tell his wives they might have interesting company that evening.

"Commander!"

Turning toward the paladin calling out to him, Raffé returned to his duties.

Island Respite

BLOOD IN THE WATER

Seree tilted his head to better enjoy the wind in his face, the fresh, salty sea air that harkened of his homeland. But though he occasionally missed the Deep, his heart was with his new home. He opened his eyes, and took in the ship they were on, sailors milling around, occasionally casting him curious looks.

Because no one quite knew what to make of Prince Aimé's beau, a mysterious man with strange knives who'd appeared out of nowhere, whisked his sister away back to nowhere, and taken up with Aimé in her place.

For a man who detested all the nonsensical drama his sisters got into, he'd done a fine job of stirring up his own.

A gentle hand rested on his back, a warm body brushing against his side. Seree turned and pulled Aimé into his arms, then tilted his head up and took a kiss. "Hello, beautiful."

That delightful flush he loved overtook Aimé's already wind-reddened cheeks. He reached up to trace the lines of Seree's scars, face full of fondness and admiration. His honest, open ways were one of the things Seree loved best about him. "No fair, that's what I wanted to say."

Seree captured his hand and kissed the palm. "Well, that would be absurd. I haven't been beautiful since I was a child, and even then I did not compare to my siblings."

"You're too hard on yourself. The first time I saw you, I could scarcely remember what I wanted to say, I was so distracted by you."

Smirking, Seree said, "It's fairly typical for people to be struck mute by the sight of a warrior of the Deep, as our presence usually means someone is in trouble."

"Oh, stop it! Take a compliment, you beautiful, aggravating man!" Aimé said with a laugh.

"Land ho!" A booming voice called out.

A short time later, they were in one of the boats taking them to the beach of a sprawling, sparkling jewel of an island, a private little escape used exclusively by the royal family when even their main island simply got to be too much. Seree would make fun of them, but his father had more castles than anyone could actually recall, except perhaps the people responsible for their maintenance.

"I'm sorry my family—" Aimé scowled as Seree placed a finger over his lips.

"Don't keep apologizing, especially about family. I have fourteen siblings and who even knows how many cousins; I know all about family. Yours just wants to make certain you're all right. I'm not sure seeing you've taken up with some scarred wild man is convincing them you are, but at least they're leaving us alone for now."

Aimé snorted softly. "I think we came all the way out here for a 'relaxing time away' to see if you'd turn into a raging, cannibalistic killer and murder us all."

"That would be a serious waste of food if I was," Seree said.

That got him a look that set him to laughing.

Aimé poked him in the stomach. "Behave!"

Seree captured his wrist and dragged him so Aimé toppled into his lap, sending all sorts of delightfully offended whispers through the boat. He kissed Aimé's nose, a warmth blossoming in his chest that he still struggled to believe was real. He struggled to believe any of this was real. Him, whose life had been fixing problems and protecting everyone else, was here with a man he loved living a life he'd never been able to admit to himself he wanted. "Where would the fun be in that? As I recall, it was misbehavior that brought me here in the first place."

That got him the sweet smile again, as Aimé twined arms around his neck and dragged him in close for a kiss. "I'm so very glad it did."

His mouth was warm and sweet, still tasting faintly of the sugared buns he'd been snacking on throughout the day. He was pliant and eager in Seree's arms, and he couldn't wait to find a bit of privacy to do all the things he wanted. "How long do you think it will take us to slip away?"

Aimé smirked, his eyes full of the same heat and eagerness consuming Seree. "As soon as we hit the beach."

"Good, because I am tired of waiting." Seree kissed him again. "I want to spread you out on a beach, or drag you into the water and wrap—" He broke off, horrified at his own words.

"Wrap…?"

"Nothing," Seree said, looking away at the faintly hurt expression on Aimé's face.

"Seree…"

Thankfully, they hit the beach then, and Aimé was distracted by the process of getting out of the boat and splashing their way to shore. "Come on." He took Seree's hand and led him further up the beach and into the jungle beyond. Shouts and protests came behind them, but Aimé ignored them, leaving Seree more than happy to do the same.

They traveled in silence for what felt like ages, trekking through the muggy jungle, focused on their path, avoiding the occasional vibrantly-colored snake or curious cluster of monkeys.

Eventually, finally, Aimé came to a stop by what proved to be an absolutely beautiful lagoon that was fed by a trio of small waterfalls, each only slightly taller than Seree. The water was so clear he could see the bottom clear as anything, like looking through glass. All around them were trees bearing mangos, bananas, and more. "It's beautiful."

"It's my favorite spot on the island. I'd come

here more often if it didn't cause the sailors such an inconvenience. They have better things to do than ferry around a single spoiled prince."

"Can't you sail?" Seree asked.

"Of course, but not alone. It would take…" His eyes widened with realization. "At least one more person to help me! A person I have now!" He threw himself into Seree's arms and kissed him soundly, fingers twining in his hair, holding Seree close, which suited him just fine.

But when they eventually pulled apart, Aimé softly asked, "What were you going to say, back on the boat?"

Seree grimaced and let him go, turned away. "Nothing. It was stupid. Something I'd do as a merman that humans, in my limited experience, would not enjoy." Especially with him, grandson of the Sea Witch, and unable to hide that legacy—in the ocean, at least. Here in the human world, nobody knew anything about him just by looking, and it was refreshingly wonderful.

"Oh," Aimee said. "Do you really think I wouldn't?" Seree turned back at the wistfulness in his voice, taken back by the longing etched plainly on his face. "I was hoping to someday see you as you really are. I mean, physically. Damn it." He sighed, closed his eyes. "I mean as a merman."

Chuckling, Seree pulled Aimé back into his arms, immediately soothed to have him so close. "I knew what you meant. Only, there are things about me I haven't told you, and I am no beautiful merman like my siblings, with a tail resembling sharks and dolphins and all manner of colorful fish. I resemble my mother, and my grandmother, and it makes me feared and loathed, despite the coloring that proves me to be my father's son."

Confusion filled Aimé's face. "I don't understand."

Seree sighed, a ball of dread filling his stomach, unpleasant knots tugging at his chest, making it ache and burn. "I suppose it is best to show you, and have done."

"I'm not going to run away screaming," Aimé snapped.

"That's what most do," Seree replied, and stepped away before he could reply, hastening down to the beach. He discarded his clothes and left them folded on a nearby rock, held down by a smaller one. Then he dove smoothly into the lagoon, and swam out until he was roughly in the middle of it, giving himself plenty of room.

He took one last look at Aimé, absorbing his beauty, his curiosity, the memory of all the kisses and torrid nights—and days—they'd shared.

Then he called up his magic, and let the reversion to his true form overtake him.

It hurt, and enduring the pain never got easier. The change tore through him like knives, or the quills of a particularly pissed off mermaid from the Sunlit Sea.

The first thing to go was his ability to breathe like a human. He could speak like one, but it took effort and practice, with vocal chords never really intended for such a use.

Next came the internal alterations, returning him to a creature that could survive the Deep, where his dinner was whatever swam by that looked tasty, and various plants that had never seen the sun. No fragrant saffron rice, or roasted garlic cream chicken, or salmon cooked in lemon and herbs, or bright vegetables smothered in butter and salt.

Once his insides were done being rearranged, the magic spread to his outside, flattening his face and taking away nearly all his nose, leeching the color from his sun-kissed skin and altering his hair to be better suited to dark, cold water. His nails turned into sharp claws, spine-tipped fins ran the length of his forearms. His ears changed, too, fins around the edges of them, adapted to hearing sounds that would never reach a human ear. His white skin was overtaken by scales that shifted from palest green around his torso to a brilliant aquamarine at the tips of his arms and where they merged into his tentacles, which were an aquamarine and teal ombre, exactly like his father's tail.

Unfortunately, the tentacles were all his mother, his grandmother. There was no hiding that he was descended from the Sea Witch, the most feared creature in the ten seas. Everyone who saw him did indeed fear him, for being a terrifying combination of Sea Witch and royal family, with the warrior scars a final blow. Spines, claws, tentacles, teeth, and venom—he was crafted for violence, and his beautiful coloring had never really been able to detract from that.

He stared hard at the water, enjoying the warmth of it, but cold inside all the same because he could not bring himself to see what Aimé now thought of him.

But the sound of splashing, swimming, jerked his head up, and he stared in bafflement as Aimé swam toward him—swam *fast*. For a human, he was impressively fluid in the water.

He'd thought Aimé would stop a few paces short, and was not prepared remotely when instead Aimé swam right up to him and practically threw himself into Seree's arms, just as he had earlier. That nearly sent them both toppling under the water, but Seree managed to keep them upright. "What in the world?" he asked, acutely aware of the arms wound tightly around his neck, the mouth just breaths away from his own.

"I was expecting something terrifying, the way you were going on. Like the weird fish that occasionally get pulled up by the fisherman, that look all melted or have weird lanterns hanging from their heads, or something like that. But you're absolutely beautiful—even more beautiful than as a human."

"I…" Seree couldn't think of what to say to that. In all his years, no one had ever called him beautiful except his parents. His sisters had as guppies, before the rest of the world taught them to be afraid of him, but no one else. Even his few lovers, always interludes that lasted days at best, always called him things like fascinating, unique, powerful. They left him feeling like a specimen they'd enjoyed playing with, rather than a person they'd enjoyed spending time with.

Aimé kissed him, mouth clear and fresh from the lagoon water. His fingers slid with easy, eager familiarity into Seree's hair, and if he cared it was thicker, and oddly slick now, he made no show of it, only kissed him harder and deeper.

Seree kissed him back fervently, tentacles coming up to tentatively hold him, waiting for that moment when Aimé recoiled, realized he was kissing a man who was really a monster.

But Aimé only shivered and clung more tightly, feeding at his mouth like he might die if he stopped.

It made Seree dizzy with relief, that Aimé still wanted him, had not yet realized just how horrifying he really was.

When they eventually drew back, Seree stared at him. With his proper eyes, colors were more vivid and beautiful than ever, bringing Aimé to life in all new ways. Seree *wanted.* His tentacles shifted restlessly in the water, his sensory arms releasing the soft, shimmery blue liquid that was essentially a lubricant. He was desperately grateful that even if Aimé noticed, he wouldn't know what it meant.

"Feels strange," Aimé said breathlessly, squirming in Seree's hold, and it was only then he realized he still had some tentacles wrapped around him. He immediately let go—and Aimé pouted of all things. "I didn't mean in a bad way." His face went suddenly scarlet, and he started to let go, pull away, and only then did Seree notice the far-from-soft cock that had been occasionally brushing against him.

Perhaps he should start paying more attention to what *was* and not bracing himself for what he expected. Aimé had *never* been what he expected, and it was part of what made him so delightful.

Seree gave in to himself, to his wants and desires, ignored those parts still quavering that he was a monster, repulsive, scary. He dragged Aimé back in close and took his mouth in a hungry, biting kiss, tentacles coming up to close around him—arms, legs, torso, keeping Aimé right where Seree wanted him: at his mercy.

He slid his attentions from Aimé's perfect mouth to kiss along his jawline, then down the delectable line of his long, beautiful throat. Aimé moaned as he tilted his head to grant better access, shivering in Seree's grasp, cock still unmistakably hard against Seree's torso. "S-Seree—"

"Yes?" Seree managed, nipping at his throat as he wrapped a tentacle around Aimé's cock, eliciting a startled cry that struck all the way to his bones and made him hungrier, needier, more possessive than ever.

That earned him even more moans, and restless, eager movements, silent pleadings for more.

Which he was more than happy to give. He used his heavy, thick, tapering tentacles to spread Aimé wide while keeping him carefully braced with head above water, and pushed a slender, straight tentacle, already slick and ready, inside him. Normally he loved to watch Aimé ride his fingers, but claw-tipped as they were right now, that just wasn't possible. But he could feel everything just fine, if not better, through the sensitive feeler tentacles that were also used in mating. Which, delightful as that could be in the Deep, he'd always enjoyed it immensely on land, too. Especially with this delightful prince whose love had broken a curse.

"Oh, gods," Aimé gasped out, almost wailing, clinging so tightly that his nails would have left divots if Seree was still human. As it was, his scales meant he barely felt it. "That feels—" He did wail that time, as Seree pushed deeper, twisted and turned just so. "Seree!"

Chuckling, low and smug and *happy*, Seree slowly and carefully added a second tentacle.

"You—" Aimé moaned again. "You're going to kill me."

Seree just continued to fuck him, bring up more tentacles to touch and tease and torment, until Aimé was reduced to a desperate, writhing bundle in his grasp, until he screamed Seree's name loud enough to startle nearby birds.

He trembled in Seree's arms as he slowly calmed, hot, panting breaths washing over his cool skin. Finally he slumped, resting his head on Seree's shoulder, one arm looped loosely around him, the other still wrapped in a tentacle.

"All right?" Seree asked softly. Would Aimé regret it, now that he'd calmed down? Would sense bring on the fear? The aversion?

Aimé gave a shaky laugh, but as he lifted his head, he looked simply as messy and flushed and happy as he always did in the aftermath of a good tumble. "More than, although I'm glad I don't have to explain my sex life to anyone because this would be tricky." He dragged Seree down into a kiss. "What about you? Did you come? I don't know how to please you in this form. It's so beautiful; I don't understand what I'm supposed to hate. You don't look like the pictures my great-grandmother painted, but I guess I don't know enough to understand why your looking different is bad. All I see is that you're absolutely stunning."

Seree kissed him for that, tangled him up close, simply savored he was there and thought Seree beautiful and desired him. Simply him. Not a prince of the Deep or a warrior of the Deep or a naughty thrill as the witch's grandson.

Drawing back, panting softly, Aimé said, "You still haven't told me what to do to get you off like this."

"You already did it," Seree said with a laugh. He wrapped one of his slender tentacles around Aimé's cock. "I do have a mating strand, as it's called, but that's only necessary for reproduction. All the fun lies with the sensory arms." He lifted a couple of them out of the water. "I most often keep them tucked away, since they're extremely sensitive and it can get distracting quickly. But this lagoon is quiet, and I like being able to feel you, even if it's akin to keeping myself semi-hard. I'm surprised you're taking it so well. But as I said earlier, there are things about me you don't know."

"That's tied to the way you look."

"Yes," Seree said with a sigh. "You know the Sea

Witch?" When he nodded, Seree added, "She's my grandmother. Her eldest daughter fell in love with my father, and I was one of three children they had together, but the only one to come out looking like my mother and grandmother. It's made me not popular in the Deep. Only the fact I have royal colors spares me. The court was never fond of my mother, they were always convinced she must be a spy or something. But she loved my father, and her children, deeply. All she ever wanted was to escape her mother. They're where I get my magical acumen as well."

"That sounds like a horrible burden to bear," Aimé said. "You can't help your birth, your family. You shouldn't be punished for things beyond your control, crimes you never committed, choices that others made. I don't understand how people can look at you and not see that you're absolutely beautiful—inside and out, human and merman. Look at what you did for your sister."

"Stole her 'true love', you mean?" Seree asked with a smile.

Aimé snickered and kissed him again. "Sorted out a mix-up, let's say."

"Something like that." Seree resumed the kissing, the touching, until Aimé was writhing in his arms again, begging and ordering and finally simply screaming before going utterly lax.

He whimpered as Seree carried him to land. "It's a good thing my family knows better than to expect me to rejoin them anytime soon."

"What do they do here? They don't really seem

the sort to enjoy roughing it."

Aimé snickered as he sprawled in the surf, completely untroubled by the tentacles wrapped around his ankles as Seree remained in the shallows, where he could still breathe through his lower set of gills, the ones high on his neck useless until he went into deeper waters. "They get drunk and say all the stuff they can't say anywhere else, about all the people they can't stand but have to deal with, that sort of thing. I like this much better."

"You prefer sex to saying mean things? Shocking."

That got him more snickering. Aimé lifted up on his elbows to better look at Seree. "What can I say? My true love is a merman of many talents."

"I'm surprised you're so eager. I would think seeing me this way would be a bit more off-putting at first."

Aimé's cheeks flushed. "When you grow up on stories of merfolk, it's inevitable that you'll wonder at some point how they do certain things."

"Certain things," Seree replied dryly. "You can just say fuck. It's what we were just doing. The whole lagoon smells of us now."

"Bet the fish don't like that."

"The fish will be fine. At least until I eat some of them. So you used to wonder how we fucked down in the Deep?"

"Did you never wonder how humans did it? Before you started coming up here?"

"I didn't have to wonder. I had lessons. They

weren't quite as accurate as I assumed, but I muddled through all right. Like to think I've gotten decent at it."

"If that's you at decent, I'll never survive you at excellent." Aimé sat up properly, naked, golden, and covered in sand. "I admit all my filthy imaginings of how merfolk fucked do not compare to the reality."

Seree's nose flared, the merman equivalent of brows shooting up. "Sounds like your imagination kept your hand quite busy."

"Quite," Aimé said with a grin. "Still not sure if I got anything right. It never occurred to me some of you came with tentacles." He wriggled his brows. "So if I asked would you tell me? Explain the difference between tentacle and non-tentacle sex in the Deep? How did your sister put it? How you sand each other?"

"No, do not learn anything from my sisters," Seree said. "That way lies trouble."

"What kind of trouble?" Aimé asked, and shrieked in delight as Seree dragged him back into the water.

Tatterlay

AN EXCEPTION

Riot's side of the bed was empty when Coroe woke up, but that wasn't really surprising. Coroe only woke early when he had no choice; Riot seemed to do it purely from habit.

Rolling out of bed, Coroe sorted through his wardrobe and finally settled on the robe his mother had given him for his most recent birthday—a soft green wool, fine as silk, and she'd embroidered it herself with white flowers and yellow dragonflies. Then he carefully brushed out his hair, and fussed over how to arrange it.

Normally he just bound it in a braid and went on with his day.

But normally he wasn't hopelessly smitten with a gorgeous man with nearly twenty years on him, who could do infinitely better than a young soldier who worked at the edge of nowhere, with nothing to recommend him but a wealthy family he rarely saw or spoke to.

Well, all right, the wealthy family was normally

more than enough to make a lot of people try to put up with him. But Riot wasn't the sort to be tempted by wealth. Thankfully, he seemed to see *something* worthwhile in Coroe.

And now that he was home, with all his clothes and jewels and such, he could really work on convincing Riot to stay with him forever.

Maybe he was getting ahead of himself. He just didn't care. Nobody had ever felt so right—in battle, in bed, in just the day to day moments.

His face flushed, heat curling through him, as thoughts of just how damn good in bed Riot was. Coroe liked to think he made a good show, but Riot left him feeling like a fumbling boy all over again.

Shoving the distracting thoughts aside, he finally braided his hair, wound it up into a crown, and finished it off with a pale wooden comb carved to look like flowers on a branch. He then pulled on his boots, buckled on his sword and bracers, and headed out.

Normally he would have needed to be up with dawn, to run morning drills, make rounds, see what the duty roster had in store for him. But Ashtor had granted him a couple days rest to settle back in after being gone for months, and Coroe was going to enjoy every second.

He'd enjoy them even more if he could find Riot, but there was no telling where he'd gotten. Coroe had introduced him to everyone at dinner last night, and they'd all teased him mercilessly for coming home with a lover, but he'd been so exhausted he barely remembered most of the evening.

So where was Riot likely to have gone? Well, he leaned toward formal, polite, and proper, so he was probably off introducing himself again to Ashtor. Last night had been more about not falling asleep in their dinner after pushing hard to reach Tatterlay.

He headed into the great hall, and sure enough, Ashtor, Riot, and Menda were sitting at one of the long tables, conversing avidly. What was Menda doing there? Usually he was long in his fields by this hour. The man lived and died for his grapes.

Coroe hesitated when he was still some paces away. They seemed like old friends, the three of them, chatting and laughing and clapping one another on the back and shoulders. They were all close in age. Unlike Coroe, who felt suddenly very much like a child.

It was fine. He and Riot had been getting along marvelously. They were bonded; nobody could compete with that.

It still felt like someone had just stabbed him in the heart with a metal wyrm spike. Was Riot realizing how much better off he'd be with someone his own age?

Then Menda glanced up, and happened to see him, breaking into a smile and lifting a hand in greeting. "There's the man himself."

Riot immediately turned, and Coroe's heartache eased at the smile that lit his face, the hand that extended. He took it, and Riot reeled him in to sit across from him, then nudged a plate toward him. "Saved you some food, since I know how much you hate sweetbuns." He motioned to a group a little further down the table, and they passed down a pitcher filled with coffee that was still hot and fresh and utterly perfect.

Coroe didn't moan as he dove into breakfast, but it was a near thing. "You're my favorite."

Ashtor laughed. "I should hope so, given you bonded with him and dragged him halfway across the continent to our boring little corner of it."

"I will take boring," Riot said. "I thought I'd miss city life more, but I already love it here."

Menda's booming laughter echoed through the hall. "You? Preferring peace and quiet? The real question is how did you survive living in a city so long?"

"I didn't hate city life, you useless drunk," Riot replied. "I liked my job, and I was good at it. But I guess I'm still a farm boy at heart, just like you can't bear to be parted from your precious wine.

Scoffing, Menda finished his coffee and rose. "I was a fighter for years. Wasn't the wine that busted my knee, you know." He retrieved his cane from where he'd laid it on the bench beside him. "If your memory is already failing, I'll be happy to regale Roe here with tales of all the times I kicked your ass."

"I'm a mage, not a fighter! Putting me in those classes was stupid." Riot waved him off. "Go away or I'll remember all the times *you* got your ass thrown around the yard."

Menda walked off laughing, cane clacking until he was out of sight.

"Why were you in fighter classes?" Coroe asked.

Riot took a sip of his coffee. "My size, of course. Everyone was certain I'd be better off a fighter, no matter my magical ability. But I honestly cannot hold a sword worth a damn, and I hate all the armor. *Hate* it. I'm more than happy to have a handsome knight do all the hard work for me." He winked.

Coroe flushed, because that was definitely a teasing reference to last night.

Next to Riot, Ashtor laughed loudly. He clapped Riot on the back briskly, nearly toppling him into his remaining coffee. "Get on then, you two. Roe, show your man around the castle. We'll talk business tonight over dinner, but I think he will definitely make a fine addition to Tatterlay." He stood and walked off, calling to nearby men to attend him.

Coroe poured more coffee and finished off the last of his sweetbuns. "I see you're settling in fine. So you and Menda know each other?"

"Classmates. Spent the night together a few times, before he met Vinna and fell over himself trying to woo her. It was hilarious. He was telling me how two of the their children have gone off to school themselves now, one to be a mage, the other to be a fighter. The third apparently shows signs of taking after the wine-obsessed side of the family."

"Milli, yeah. I swear she already knows as much as him, and she's only twelve. You and Menda were lovers?" Coroe couldn't wrap his head around the thought. It was too weird.

Riot gave him a look, mouth quirked in amusement. "Does that bother you?"

"Bother? Not the way you're probably thinking," Coroe replied. "It's almost impossible to think of Menda with anyone but Vinna, for one. For two, it's like trying to picture my lover with my uncle." Coroe shuddered. "So I'd rather not think about it, thanks. Would you like the grand tour, now you've teased me in front of my boss and made me think gross things about Menda?"

Riot laughed and stood up, stretching as he did, presenting a delightful distraction to cleanse Coroe's mind. "Come here and I'll make it better."

Oh, Coroe was helpless to do anything but obey when Riot used that husky, full-of-promise voice. He abandoned his coffee and leapt neatly over the table, landing right beside Riot. "I'm here."

"So you are," Riot said, and threaded his fingers into the hair at Coroe's nape, eliciting shivers of delighted anticipation before he took Coroe's mouth. His kiss was warm and flavored of coffee, but far better at waking Coroe up. They were nearly the same height, Riot just the barest bit taller. He was big enough to be practically two of Coroe, but his touch was always gentle. The jewels in his wrists tingled wherever they brushed against Coroe's skin.

He drew back, touching his tongue to his top lip just to savor the taste of Riot that lingered there. Gods, it would never stop being the greatest thrill, how the jewels he wore matched Coroe's eyes. He was marked *Property of Coroe, Besotted Knight* and Coroe would do whatever it took to keep it that way.

"What's put your head up in the clouds?" Riot

asked, mouth ticking up at the corner. As in everything, his tells were soft, quiet, and contained. More than once when they'd first met, Coroe had misread him as being upset, or at least indifferent. Now, he didn't know how he'd missed a thousand little clues.

Coroe laughed and twined his arms around Riot's neck. "I was just being a possessive ass, admiring for the ten thousandth time how good you look with your stones matched to me."

"I see," Riot said, but the gleam in his eyes betrayed his pleasure. "You're lucky you're cute when you're being a possessive ass."

"I'm cute when I do everything."

Riot's mouth curved into a positively evil grin. "I can think of a few times where 'cute' is not the word I'd use."

"Stop that!" Coroe let go and gave him a playful shove that didn't move Riot one bit. "I can't believe you teased me like that right in front of His Lordship."

"You made it too easy. Now are you going to show me around the grounds, or shall I keep teasing you right here where we have a growing audience?"

Coroe gave him a look, but offered a hand and thrilled quietly when Riot took it without hesitation. "Come on, then. I'll show you my favorite spot in the whole of Tatterlay." He grinned briefly. "It might even afford privacy for a bit of revenge on my mage."

"Sounds promising."

Coroe secured them a couple of horses, and then they were riding out into the quieter stretches of

Tatterlay, filled with endless fields of crops, mills to grind many of them, silos, and more. It was a small territory, largely overlooked, but it was strong and thriving. When Coroe had first agreed to come, he'd worried he'd find it boring after a life filled with cities and merchant trains and school halls, but it was just busy enough to keep him engaged without bleeding him dry.

Past all the fields, houses, and sheds, the territory turned to forest that made good hunting and also provide a natural wall to mark Tatterlay, which ended where the forest stopped.

Coroe led them deep into it woods, along a path that barely qualified as such, the sound of a waterfall steadily increasing, until they spilled into a clearing, where a waterfall roughly as high as three men spilled into a beautiful pond of cool, crisp water. Coroe had found the place by chance one day, hunting a gray bear that had had somehow slipped through the wards from the Territories.

He'd returned on purpose another day, and many days since. It was his private retreat from the world, a place he'd shared with no one else.

"Come on," he said, dismounting and leaving his horse to happily graze.

Riot gave him a curious look, but remained silent and obediently followed as Coroe led him around the western edge of the pond, up some slippery rocks, and then behind them to walk along a tiny path between boulders, until they were able to slip behind the waterfall itself.

Where there was a little cave, which Coroe had painstakingly worked to make comfortable. He'd hauled in bedding, the hay to stuff it, blankets and pillows to make into a cozy nest. There were mage lights, a trunk of foodstuffs, another of extra bedding and changes of clothes, books and his old pipes, spare weapons. The makings of a chair were set neatly in one corner, the project about half done, the little table to go with it already finished, a twin to the one already by the bed.

"This is beautiful," Riot said, and at his gentle touch, the mage lights flared brighter, taking on a soft blue tone. "How did you do all this?"

Sitting on the edge of the bed, Coroe removed his boots, weapons, and out layers as he explained, and then climbed up to sprawl comfortably. "Come and join me."

"If you insist." Riot removed his own shoes and outer layers before joining him, immediately pulling Coroe into a kiss. He went easily when Coroe pushed him into the bedding and sprawled across him, hands coming up to cup and fondle Coroe's ass. "I see you've already memorized one of my weaknesses."

"Is that the secret cave, the lying around in the middle of the day, or that you like when I ride you?"

Riot's eyes glittered. "Maybe I should amend that to 'a few of my weaknesses'. Though I sense they can all just be summed up as you." He pulled Coroe into a kiss, one hand curving around the back of his neck, holding him at just the right angle for a mind-melting kiss that left Coroe whimpering, aching.

They made short work of their clothes after that, and Coroe withdrew only to fetch the jar of lubricant he kept in a basket by the bed.

"I see you come here with a particular purpose in mind," Riot said with a laugh. "Do I need to worry about lovers popping in at awkward moments?"

Coroe laughed, though it turned into a stuttered moan as Riot wrapped a hand around his cock. "I'm the only one who comes here. You're the first person I've brought."

Something flashed, hot and bright, in Riot's eyes, and then Coroe suddenly found himself in Riot's place, one of the pillows falling across his face. He threw it aside impatiently, and was met with another of those searing, toe-tingling kisses, the hand returning to his cock, slick this time, and far too good at what it did.

"Riot…" Coroe pulled restlessly at the bedding.

Riot's husky laugh washed over him, doing nothing to lessen his need. "Do you need something?"

"Stop being a bastard and fuck me already."

"Youth. So impatient." Riot let go of his cock and shifted so he could trail his mouth all over Coroe's skin—jaw, throat, collarbone, lingering at Coroe's nipples, which had always been happy for whatever attention they could receive. Riot bit one firmly, and Coroe thrust up, groaning and trembling. "You remind me of this whore I spent a few nights with once, when I was first traveling to Gravington's castle. She had hoops in her nipples, and a chain that connected them."

Coroe shuddered. "No way. I'd feel them all the

time under my armor and would never get anything done ever again. I would jerk my cock until it fell off."

Riot laughed and laughed, until Coroe grabbed a handful of hair and shoved him pointedly back to work. In revenge, Riot sucked up a mark on his hip, right where his sword belt would press against it, drive him mad even through layers of cloth and leather.

The divine torment continued until Coroe was so desperate and aching he couldn't form words anymore, just lie there trembling and moaning. Only then did Riot slide into him, and fuck him with steady, deep strokes that had Coroe coming apart just minutes later.

Riot followed him a short time later, sinking in deep and filling the cavern with his deep groan before slumping on top of Coroe, heavy and sweaty and utterly delightful. Coroe kissed one damp cheek. "Not bad, old man."

Cracking an eye open, Riot glared half-heartedly. "Quit that."

Coroe laughed and shifted until they lay side by side, still marvelously tangled together, the cool air from the waterfall wafting over them. "I'm glad you like Tatterlay so far."

"Me too," Riot replied. "It would have been vexing to come all this way only to hate it." He winked, and skated his hands lazily over Coroe's skin. "I admit, though, my relief is mostly that nobody seems to mind you came home trailing a besotted old man."

"Ashtor is friends with Lord Jenohn, you know."

"The Jenohn? The one bonded and married to

Lord Selsor?" Riot gaped. "That's incredible. I've always wanted to meet Lord Selsor; he's a legend in more ways than one."

"Well, you may get your chance, eventually. Ashtor is always trying to get Jenohn to come see him. But my point was that Ashtor has seen what their bonding does, the positive effect it's had on the places where it's already spread. So he's probably ecstatic to have a bonded pair here, and is going to put us to work ensuring the practice spreads. Ashtor is always plotting. He loves scheming and planning more than anything else in the world. I will die of shock if he ever settles down with someone."

"Speaking of settling down…"

Coroe's heart dropped into his stomach. "What?"

"Stop looking like you're going to your execution, good grief," Riot said. "Ashtor said that if we wanted more space than your current room, that there's plenty of room in the castle proper, and he'd be happy to have us."

"Oh, room in the fancy castle. Guess you are good to have around."

"Brat."

"You're the one who bonded to me," Coroe replied.

Riot's smile was full of warmth and fondness. No one had ever looked at Coroe in such a way, not outside his parents, and it wasn't the same thing at all. "Yes, I did."

The Professor and the Gambler

THE MATCHMAKER

Lyle stood in the hallway just outside Jocelyn's office, feeling like someone had turned his whole world upside down.

The old doubts tried to rekindle, but they were no match for Jocelyn's logic, his stupid logic that should have occurred to Lyle forever ago.

And all the other little things he'd said.

Eustace had never slept with Sorrel. Eustace wanted *him*, boring, stodgy, thirty-five going on seventy Lyle.

Could it really be true? His heart was pounding so rapidly, so hard, that Lyle was half-afraid it would explode. Eustace might care for him romantically. Did he dare find out, once and for all?

But he'd lingered and sulked and wallowed in misery long enough. Even if Jocelyn was wrong, it was long past time to put the matter to rest and move on.

Gods, though, would his heart shatter into a

thousand pieces if he'd just gotten his hopes up for nothing, after years of hopeless pining.

He paused in front of one of the many hallway mirrors to fuss with his clothes and hair, try to make himself a little more elegant lord and a little less frumpy professor. A lost cause, likely, but at least he'd tried.

As ready as he would ever be, he went in search of Eustace, who naturally proved to be nigh impossible to find that day. Not in his office. Not in his favorite salon playing with his cards. Lyle scoured the whole of the palace, and could find him nowhere.

Ready to scream, or possibly even cry, with frustration, he headed off to his own chambers before he did something stupid. It was fine. He'd see Eustace eventually. The conversation had waited this long, it could wait a few hours, or god forbid days, more.

But when he turned the corner and headed down the hall to his room, he spied a figure sitting on one of the benches lining the hall. He stuttered to a halt as he realized it was Eustace. "Have you been here the whole time?"

"I wanted a word with you," Eustace said, slowly standing.

Lyle laughed, because otherwise he would scream. "I've been looking all over the palace for you."

Eustace stared at him, then laughed as well. "I'm sorry. I suppose we should have remember that things like sending a note exist." The laughter faded into an anxious smile. "What did you want to speak to me about?"

"Let's adjourn to my chambers, shall we? Instead of speaking out here in the hall." When Eustace nodded, Lyle unlocked his door and led the way inside. He shrugged out of his jacket and removed his neckcloth, finding both abruptly stifling.

Eustace did the same, and it did nothing at all to keep Lyle from thinking about how badly he'd always wanted to find and kiss every freckle on his beautiful body. "Let's have it then."

"First, I wanted to say I'm sorry. You've insisted all these years that you and Sorrel were never amorous, and instead of believing you as I should have I just assumed you were lying, even though it's never been in your nature to lie about such things, and it's not Sorrel's nature to bed his friends."

Surprise filled Eustace's face, and then a smile the likes of which Lyle had never seen. "What finally compelled you to believe me?"

Lyle sighed. "I hate that it took anyone to make me stop being a complete fool, but I confess it was a conversation with the Matchmaker. He is damned good at his job, as much as it pains me to admit it."

"He is," Eustace said, smiling faintly. "I admit I rather like the bastard, as much as I've tried not to. Though part of his charm is that he is getting to Sorrel in a way I've never seen. I daresay Sorrel is smitten, and does not like the feeling at all."

"Sorrel? Dislike not being completely and utterly in control of himself and his surroundings? Being at the mercy of another? Never say," Lyle drawled, and smiled when Eustace laughed.

As the laughter faded, Eustace said, "Does this mean we can go back to being friends the way we were? I've missed you, and how easy it used to be between us. I swear to you it's never even crossed my mind to tangle sheets with Sorrel. It'd be like bedding an angry cat who is also my brother."

Lyle took a deep breath, braced himself for the worst, and said, "To be honest, I don't want to go back to the way we were."

Eustace's face fell. "What do you mean?"

"I mean—" Lyle broke off, nerves getting the better of him. "That is, I know there is some gap in our ages and you were once a student while I was a professor, and—" He stopped again, then sighed loud and long. "I am botching this entirely." Meeting Eustace's bewildered gaze, he mustered every scrap of courage he possessed and said, "You must be the only person unaware that I am madly in love with you, and have been seething with jealousy all this time that it was Sorrel who won your affections."

"Madly—" Eustace stared at him, mouth agape, and then abruptly lunged forward, nearly knocking them both to the floor, but before Lyle could ask what he was about, Eustace was wrapped quite firmly around him and kissing him like a man possessed.

Lyle was many things, a complete fool among them, but he had enough sense to wrap his arms tightly around Eustace's waist and return the kiss with equal fervor. Eustace tasted like raspberries and tea, like basking in the sun on a summer day. He was perfect. Better than. Everything Lyle had ever dreamed of and more.

When they finally drew apart, he could only stare into Eustace's hazel eyes, share panting breaths.

It was Eustace who finally broke the silence. "I've always felt the same, you know. Madly. But I assumed you always saw me as... well, the poor student who got beat up for calling out cheaters and couldn't even afford his own medical care. Young. Foolish. A reckless gambler."

Lyle brushed a soft kiss across his mouth, then drew back enough to say, "All I ever saw was a beautiful, determined and outgoing young man who could have the world, and would never want to settle for a boring, predictable professor already quite set in his ways."

"You're a fool," Eustace said, and kissed him again, while also driving him back, until Lyle broke away with a yelp as he toppled down onto his sofa. Before Lyle could recover, Eustace was straddling him and diving right back into feasting at his mouth.

Lyle had only had one other lover of note, and even he had never shown half the enthusiasm that Eustace put into a single kiss. It was heady. Enthralling. Lyle was never letting Eustace escape.

When they drew apart to catch their breath, Lyle nearly came right then and there at the sight of Eustace's flushed face, mussed hair, the well-used lips that were entirely Lyle's doing. "I can't believe you want me."

"Lyle, I've been half in love with you since the night you saved me, and wholly in love since not long after that. How could I not be?"

"How could you, is the question I always asked myself over the years, and I could never devise an answer."

Eustace kissed him, soft and sweet and devastating. "You have a heart of sunshine, you're brilliant and funny, the entire student body worships you… I could go on for ages, you nitwit. You're my dearest friend, even when you were being a jealous ass."

Lyle winced. "I am sorry. I should have believed you. But it seemed wholly logical in my head that you would fall for someone as compelling and beautiful as Sorrel."

"Only if I wanted to get frostbite," Eustace replied, and nuzzled against him. "I want you, nitwit. Just you."

"You have me."

Eustace's eyes glittered. "Not yet I don't." He squirmed from Lyle's lap, leaving him aching and groaning, and sank to his knees in front of him. Lyle's breath lodged in his throat as Eustace's deft, elegant fingers worked at the fastenings of his breeches. He'd watched Eustace's hands more times than he could count, as he rolled dice or played with his beloved cards, or sometimes toyed with a coin, rolling and spinning and catching it.

He never thought he'd see those same hands pulling out his cock, stroking and teasing it, until Lyle was so hard he hurt. "Not that I'm complaining, but aren't we going rather fast?"

"I've waited a long damn time for this," Eustace said. "I'm not waiting one second more." With that, he dropped his mouth over Lyle's cock, suckling briefly at the tip before taking him deeper, until he touched the back of Eustace's throat. His cheeks hollowed as he sucked in earnest, tongue rubbing wonderfully over ever bit it could reach.

Lyle's ability to think vanished entirely. All he could do was comb through Eustace's hair, mussing it completely, and work his hips gently, fucking into that hot, eager mouth, moaning Eustace's name between bouts of showering praise over him. For that mouth. Those lust-bright eyes. The eagerness and talent. How absolutely beautiful he was, especially right then, on his knees, mouth stuffed full, the world reduced to just the two of them and all the pleasure they could give each other.

He came groaning Eustace's name, spilling down his throat, fingers sunk into his hair. When Eustace finally pulled away, gently suckling as he went, Lyle could have come again. If he'd thought Eustace mussed from his kisses was arousing, it had nothing on Eustace utterly wrecked from sucking him, face red from exertion, smeared with spit and come, lips so swollen he half-feared they were bruised.

Lyle shoved him to the floor, made quick work of his breeches, and finally got hold of Eustace's cock. "I fervently hope you'll be willing to fuck me at a later time. For now my hand will have to suffice."

Eustace just moaned and thrust up into his touch, one arm draped over his eyes, the other scrabbling at the carpet for purchase as he moved in time with Lyle's firm strokes. He wished he'd thought to bring lubricant of some sort, but hadn't even dreamed they would go this far so immediately. So he made do with what he had available. Thankfully, Eustace seemed disinclined to complain.

It took only moments for him to come, spilling over Lyle's hand warm and sticky. Watching his face as he came was a gift from the divine. Lyle wanted to see it again and again. "You're even more beautiful when I have you under me."

"Wait until you get me naked," Eustace said with a smile, the words coming out between soft pants. "Though I'm looking forward to having you under me while I make you scream."

Lyle groaned, cock trying to twitch back to life. "I'm going to need more time if you want a rise out of me."

"Well what say we get naked and climb into bed in the meantime?" Eustace asked, and climbed to his feet. What a sight that was—disheveled clothes, face and hair still a complete mess, cock shamelessly hanging out. Lyle's cock twitched again, and he thought it might not take that long at all for him to ready for a second round.

He climbed to his own feet and stripped off his shirt, then sat to work on his shoes and stockings. By the time he'd risen to strip off his breeches and smallclothes, Eustace was already delightfully naked, and more beautiful than all of Lyle's illicit imaginings.

Stepping close, he ran a hand along Eustace's

chest, smooth and toned, nothing at all like his own soft, slightly squishy frame, the result of spending more time with books or at his desk and lectures halls than doing anything healthful. "You're more beautiful than I can find words to describe." He couldn't believe this was real.

But there was no denying the heat of Eustace's mouth as he drew Lyle into a kiss, the warm press of his body as he held Lyle tight. The huskiness of his voice, and the lust in his eyes as he said, "Take me to bed, professor."

"No, do not start that," Lyle said, shoving him away before turning and heading off to his bedroom.

Snickering followed him, and there was a quick pinch to his ass that made Lyle yelp. "But professor, I'm eager for whatever instruction you're willing to provide."

"Stop it!" Lyle said, torn between laughter and groaning. "You'll just make it worse when the invariable rumors of what we did while you were still a student begin." He reeled Eustace in and deposited him on the bed before getting the half-empty jar from his bedside table and climbing into bed himself.

Eustace gazed at him through his lashes, contriving the most ridiculous pout. "As you wish, professor."

Lyle swatted his thigh, leaving a faint handprint, making Eustace jump—and his cock twitch. Lyle's brow quirked. "Just misbehaving for the discipline, are you? Eager to be a bad student?"

"Maybe some other time," Eustace said, turning

red. "But if I can't make professor/student jokes, neither can you. Now come here."

Lyle swatted him again, this time on the ass, just because he could, then let a flushed and embarrassed Eustace drag him into bed and distract him. "I suppose I can allow it from time to time. Try to be a good student for now and fuck me."

"Yes, professor," Eustace said, a wicked gleam in his eye. He'd cleaned his face at some point, though his lips were still red and swollen, and his hair a hopeless tangle.

To Lyle's delight and dismay, Eustace only sort of obeyed, putting his mouth to every bit of Lyle's skin he could easily reach, leaving a mark low on his throat where no one would see it, but Lyle would certainly feel it as his clothes rubbed against it.

He kissed Lyle's arms, nipped and licked his chest, put teeth to one hipbone and dragged them across his stomach. Then he pressed a single, teasing kiss to Lyle's hard cock before shifting attention to the soft, inner skin of his thighs, where he left more marks that would be sure to torment him later.

"You're a brat," Lyle gasped out as Eustace finally turned back to his cock.

"I am going to indulge in as many of my fantasies as I possibly can, before you realize you could do better and change your mind."

"I could not do better if a king offered me his whole kingdom," Lyle said, and groaned as Eustace licked a strip up the length of his cock. "Fuck me, now. I want to come with you inside me."

Eustace groaned and grabbed his cock. "Don't say stuff like that." He snatched up the jar Lyle had left nearby and hastily slicked himself before working one slick finger into Lyle's hole.

"Just fuck me, I can take it," Lyle said. "I'm well-used to availing myself of sexual devices."

That got him another of those long groans, muffled as Eustace buried his head in the hollow of Lyle's throat, a full-body shudder running through him, cock jerking against Lyle's skin. He drew back after a moment, kissed Lyle hard, leaving his lips throbbing, and then slowly slid inside him. It stretched and burned in the best way, exactly as Lyle liked it, but a thousand times better because it was Eustace rather than one of his toys.

He held on tight, wrapping his arms around Eustace, clinging to his sweaty back, panting and pleading as Eustace thrust into him over and over, needing release but wanting the moment to last forever.

Between thrusts, Eustace gasped out, "I want to do this every day. Fifty times a day."

Lyle laughed, but it turned into a shout as Eustace thrust into him one last time, hard and deep, and his climax rushed over him. He only barely felt it as Eustace followed shortly after, and was still catching his breath when Eustace pulled out and rolled to sprawl out beside him.

"So do I pass muster, professor?" Eustace asked.

"Stop that, I'm serious," Lyle said with a groan, pressing the heels of his hands to his eyes. "You're such a brat, how did I forget that?"

"You were distracted, I'd wager." Eustace rolled over to sprawl on Lyle's chest. "So am I finally able to tell the world that you're my lover?"

"Most certainly," Lyle said, and kissed him softly before settling in for a nap.

Beloved Regent

THE ENGINEERED THRONE

Vellem picked up his coffee and sighed at himself when it proved to still be empty. You'd think by the third time he'd remember that, but this was four and he'd probably hit six before he got it through his head.

Normally there were servants ghosting about, keeping his desk ordered and his coffee filled, their ability to go about silent and unseen vastly outstripping his best scouting teams. Right then, though, everyone was busy preparing for the arrival of Princess Akari, and frankly with that weighing constantly at the back of his mind, Vellem preferred to be left alone.

Even if it meant he kept running out of coffee.

Sighing, he gave up on the letter he'd been attempting to write and pushed away from his desk, stretching and groaning as he stood. Rubbing at his stiff neck, he grabbed up his empty cup and headed off to the antechamber in search of a refill.

But when he stepped through the door, he was

greeted not with the sight of clerks, but all four of his generals, who'd clearly been on their way into the office. Vellem's brows rose. "Why do I sense an ambush?"

Malla grinned and replied, "Because you're a veteran who knows what he's about."

"I don't think I ever actually was discharged," Vellem replied. "Can I refill my coffee before you full troublemakers foist your mischief upon me?"

"I suppose we'll allow it," drawled Desten.

His remaining two generals, Carmen and Ordan, made a feeble attempt at muffling their snickers.

Vellem rolled his eyes, went over to the clerk's desk, and thanked her as she refilled his mug from the pot she kept behind the desk. "Come on, then. Bev, see we're not disturbed until these miscreants leave."

"Yes, Majesty," she replied with a laugh.

In his office, vacant save for himself and a couple of secretaries not commandeered by Perdith as he focused on the pending royal visit, he leaned against his desk, set his coffee aside after a couple of generous swallows, and folded his arms across his chest. "Let's have it, then."

Malla stepped forward and offered a small packet of papers, affixed with the royal seal and Perdith's elegant signature. "His Majesty says he is happy to make this official, but only with your approval/permission. So we have come to bully you into doing our bidding. Majesty."

Vellem's brows rose as he took the papers and

started skimming—then stopped and went back to read it properly. His eyes widened, and he didn't even bother to finish reading the royal order before tossing it on his desk. "Absolutely not."

That got him a chorus of protests like he'd just told all the enlisted their leave was canceled indefinitely.

"Enough, enough," Vellem said, holding up his hands.

Malla pouted at him, like she was girl instead of his best and most ruthless general. "But you have to agree. We've been working on this for ages, and it would mean the world to us and the rest of the army."

Vellem groaned. "I do not want a military medal named after my ridiculous epithet."

"But it would be so inspiring, empowering. It would mean so much to so many," Desten said.

Carmen added, "You have to stop acting like you don't know you're looked on as a hero by everyone—military *and* civilian, titled and common, native and foreign—for your actions after the Tragedy. People want to honor you, and see that what you did lives on, becomes inspiration for others to always aim to act with the same—"

"Stop it," Vellem hissed, face hot. "I didn't do anything special. I acted as anyone would in my position. I had duties and responsibilities and I worked to fulfill them, that's all."

"No, Majesty," Ordan said quietly, her voice quiet but forceful. "You could have run back to Belemere. You could have ensured that Perdith never woke up. Become a tyrant. Sold us out to literally any other country on the continent. We were vulnerable in a thousand ways, one step away from falling apart and being conquered, and were very literally saved by a man who barely knew our customs and was enduring pain and tragedies of his own. Maybe to you it's just 'what anyone would have done' but that only speaks further to your character, to the depths of your heart. Many people in your position would have acted very differently—selfishly."

"I wasn't entirely selfless you know," Vellem replied. "Let's be honest: there was nothing for me to return to in Belemere, not really. My best chance at the life I wanted was right here, even if it came with more responsibility than I'd been prepared for. Hardly altruistic."

"Oh, quit it," Malla said. "You were regarded highly in Belemere, and you're regarded even more highly here. Since I doubt you'll ever let anyone build a statue of you—"

"Absolutely not!" Vellem said, terror and mortification sliding down his spine. He just wanted to be a good consort, prove himself worthy every day to be at Perdith's side and care for all the people relying on him. "If you ever dare suggest such a thing I will put you in stone shoes, Lain, do you understand me?"

Malla and the others just laughed.

Carmen was still grinning as the laughter faded. "I would just like to point out that nobody needs your permission to commission a statue of you. So if you sign those papers and let us do this one small thing, then we promise no statues will go up until after you're ashes in the wind. If you keep being stubborn..."

Vellem groaned, but he knew a defeat when he saw one. Going around his desk, he sat down, opened his bottom drawer, and poured himself a generous swallow of the bottle of good whiskey he kept there to enjoy at the end of particularly trying days.

He drank it one smooth shot, then dragged the papers over and read them over again, sighing heavily. "I really don't like this, miscreants."

They all smiled like children trying to assure their father they would never, ever get into mischief, they promised. Malla said, "But it will make your subjects happy, Your Majesty, and we all know that's your greatest weakness. After our king, anyway."

Vellem gave them a look, sighed heavily, and finally signed the papers, pressing his seal as Commander-in-Chief of the Royal Army and Navy of Tallideth, making it official that the highest possible medal that a soldier could receive for valor and gallantry in the line of duty was the Royal Medal of the Unbreakable Soldier.

"There," he said. "Now if you'll excuse me, I have a husband to go berate for being party to this."

Their snickering followed him out of the office, leaving Vellem rolling his eyes, but also with a smile tugging at his mouth. In the antechamber, he motioned to some of the stationed guards. "I am going in search of my husband, if you would not mind keeping me company."

He would never grow entirely used to the need

for bodyguards, but he couldn't deny that he had an extensive history of attempted assassinations.

The bodyguards fell in around and behind him, one several paces ahead to clear the way when necessary.

Thankfully, it wasn't hard to find Perdith, who was in the new, still un-used ballroom, which was awaiting a special commemoration ball taking place in a few days—the other reason for the chaos, since the ball was just two days before the arrival of Princess Akari.

"A word with my husband, please," Vellem said as he reached the cluster of people that perpetually surrounded Perdith these days, a combination of secretaries, clerks, nobles wanting his attention, and staff needing his attention. When a few looked like they wanted to protest, Vellem gave them the look that sent soldiers scurrying.

The ballroom was cleared of all but the two of them in a matter of minutes. Perdith chuckled softly as the closing of the door echoed through the vast, empty space.

It had been beautifully rebuilt, all white, cream, and blue, with a rainbow mosaic in the floor and a painting over the royal dais—designed to be open beneath so nothing could be hidden beneath it again—that was a memorial to the fallen. Perdith had named it after his sister, the late crown princess, and the entire new east wing after his mother. The new garden was named after his nieces and nephews who'd been killed in the blast. Even now, Vellem couldn't think about it too hard or he'd still get angry that anyone would do something like that to *children.*

"What word would you like to have with me?" Perdith asked, twining arms around his neck and tilting his head in an invitation older than time.

Vellem accepted it gladly, sliding arms around Perdith's trim waist and bending down slightly to kiss that soft, warm mouth he knew as well as his own. He could live a thousand years and never grow tired of kissing Perdith.

When he was finally able to tear himself away, he murmured, "Why in the Moons did you permit that stupid medal?"

Perdith burst into laughter. "They finally mustered the nerve to speak with you?"

"Mustered the nerve? They said they were going to bully me into it and practically did!" Vellem gave Perdith a playful shake and let him go.

"I signed that paperwork nearly a week ago. Trust me, they've been nervous about approaching you."

Vellem shook his head. "Why on earth would they be nervous?"

Perdith gave him a fond, amused look. "Because they look up to you just as much as everyone else around this place, and they were deathly afraid you'd be angry and refuse to do it. That medal means everything to them, it's become their Project. Are you truly that unhappy about it?"

"Just flustered like always," Vellem replied. "I'm not even half as remarkable as everyone insists I am.

You know that better than anyone."

"I know no such thing," Perdith said, wrapping around him again, pressing a soft kiss to his mouth, and then his throat. "Nobody in the world loves and admires you more than me." He drew back slightly, eyes sparkling with mirth and promise. "If you'll come along to inspect the new coat room with me, I'll demonstrate my admiration."

Vellem went easily as Perdith dragged him along, anticipation pooling low and hot in his gut. "As my king wishes."

Man of the Hour
GORGON BOY

"Stop feeding my hair!" Siri hissed.

Miranda just gigged and gave one of the little bastards another piece of her club sandwich. Siri hated it when people treated his hair like pets; it was weird as hell feeling the food they ate creep down the back of his head into his throat.

"Come on, quit it, they don't need it and I don't like it," Siri said when she did it yet again.

"Fine, fine, sorry. They're just so cute."

Siri sighed and tried to go back to reading over the papers she'd brought him to look over.

Though he was trying to remain all cool and collected, act like the functional adult he theoretically was, inside he wanted to jump around in excitement. After years of school and gaining experience and getting everything in order, he was finally going to open his private tutoring school for all the overlooked paranormal kids in town.

All around him, his snakes wriggled and squirmed, sharing his excitement. They'd grown long over the years, halfway down his chest at this point, but even though they'd be perfectly fine with a chop-chop, it was still too gruesome and messy an undertaking for him to bring himself to do it.

"I don't think I've ever seen you look so excited," Miranda said. "You're so self-contained, except for your hair. It's cute."

"I'm not cute," Siri replied automatically as he finished reading over the papers and started signing. Most of them were for the building he was leasing, a negotiation that had taken months because the landlord was a stubborn, greedy asshole trying to commit fricking highway robbery, but it was done. The rest of the papers were to get the ball rolling on making the building suitable: classrooms, study rooms, a cafeteria, offices, and more.

"Seriously, you're cute."

"Shut up," Siri mumbled.

Miranda just giggled some more, making him smile. He wouldn't have come as far as he had without her, the best damn lawyer in town. "So are you going to have—" She broke off and whistled. "Wow, check out that hottie gargoyle."

Surprise and delight ran through Siri, and he turned in his seat to see that his husband was in fact coming straight toward them. He leapt out of his seat. "Hal!"

Hal broke into an absolutely beautiful smile and hastened his step, catching Siri up into a hug and spinning him around like the giant goober he was.

Siri threw arms around his neck and kissed him

soundly. "You're home early!"

"Couple of students had to come back early for a family emergency, so we just wrapped up early and all came home. We'll go back in the spring, probably. I hear congratulations are in order." He slowly let go of Siri, and reached up to stroke and pet the snakes that immediately started fussing over him. After a moment, his attention shifted. "You must be the marvelous Miranda I've heard so much about."

"It's a pleasure to meet you!" Miranda said, leaping to her feet and smoothing out her smart skirt and blazer before offering a hand to shake. "Your goofball never mentioned you were a gargoyle."

Siri grinned unrepentantly. "A *hottie* gargoyle."

"Shut up." Miranda elbowed him out of the way. "So you're a professor, right? History, if I recall, though I don't remember your specialty."

"Gargoyle society of the mid-fourteenth century, more or less," Hal said with a smile. "It started as just interest in my personal family history, but now I get paid to research them and others. I was going to take Siri out to celebrate the lease signing. Did you want to join us?"

Miranda shook her head. "Maybe we can do lunch tomorrow, but no way would I interrupt you spoiling your ridiculous gorgon here. The snakes would never forgive me." She fed one of them a last remaining shred of bacon from her sandwich. "I'll take care of these and see you tomorrow, Siri. Take care, and congrats again!" She kissed his cheek, gathered her stuff, and sauntered off, heels clicking, figure drawing more than a few pairs of eyes.

"She seems nice," Hal said.

"She is." Siri cuddled in close, breathing in the familiar warm, summery scent that he'd missed so badly the past two months. "I can't believe you're home almost a whole month early." His snakes moved all about his head, tangling up in each other as they wrestled each other to touch Hal, who just chuckled and pet them all as best he could, unconcerned at the way they wound and wrapped around his arms.

It was a good thing Siri didn't mind being literally tangled up in Hal, because he wasn't going anywhere any time soon. Later, in bed, his stupid hair would be even more ridiculous. "I think my snakes like you better than me."

Hal chuckled and nuzzled his cheek before kissing him softly again. "That's not true. They just know you have a little bit of a thing for me."

"But only a little bit," Siri said with a smile.

"Honestly, I should have figured out sooner that you liked me back, given how often they were always trying to touch me and stuff."

"You really should have." Siri kissed him again, then started pulling snakes apart, managing to step back with minimal fuss. "So are you actually taking me to dinner, or are we just going to go home and fuck like we're still in college?"

Hal's eyes were hot with anticipation and promise. "You're the man of the hour, darling. What do you want?"

"I want my sexy husband to take me home and

show me how much he's missed me, and then we'll go to dinner. Maybe. Depends on how thoroughly you wear me out."

That got him the hot little growly noise that he loved more than life, before Hal swept him up like the heroine in a movie and carried him off to the car, snakes wriggling all around them in delighted anticipation.

Forest Frolic

RASNAKE

Cecil threw aside the last of his filthy clothes and plunged into the bracing stream, nearly unbalancing at the post-storm current but holding steady at the last. Shivering, he plunged beneath the water to get the worst over with, then surfaced and raked his hair from his face.

Fetching his soap from where he'd tossed it and other items on a rock in the middle of the stream, he set to scouring away sweat, dirt, and other grime from a long day in the woods rousting out any possible dragon nests. They'd found two, but one had been overtaken by bears and the other hadn't been used in months.

Nearby, Bite and Raze had finished their own bath and were lolling indolently on the bank, tongues out, faces full of happiness and contentment as they soaked up the sunshine.

Cecil smiled faintly as he set to work on his hair, pulling it out of the simple braid he'd put it in for working, scrubbing and combing until it was as tidy as it would ever get.

That taken care of, he worked on shaving next, and when that was done started on one last, thorough soaping down.

He was just rinsing off when the wolves rose to attention, but with a relaxed, even excited demeanor. Just as Cecil turned, a voice said, "What have we here? A delightful dryad just waiting to be seduced by an elf?"

Cecil rolled his eyes, but laughed as he watched Tallant approach the bank of the stream. "Hardly a dryad, and I don't think it's called seducing when it's your lover. I think that's just called having a lover."

He realized his mistake the moment Tallant's eyes took on that familiar gleam. "Would you like me to have you, kel? Or would you like to have me?"

"Shut up," Cecil said, hating that even after all these months, his face still got hot at the ridiculous things Tallant said. Growing up, he'd always imagined himself as a skilled, smart, witty lover who made all the innuendo. But imagination and reality were, as ever, leagues apart. He would always be a failed scholar turned killer turned awkward in-between, in love with the most obnoxious elf ever born.

Tallant just continued smirking, and crooked a finger.

"No," Cecil retorted. "I do not exist to do your bidding. I'm trying to get clean, not get dirt in uncomfortable places *again*. Never mind the damn spiders."

Making a face, Tallant replied, "Now why did

you have to bring that up?"

"Keeps you humble."

"Not even my mother could instill humility." Tallant stripped off his equipment and armor, then his tunics. When he was bare from the waist up, he sat to pull off his boots, casting them aside before standing once more to discard the rest of his clothes.

Any thoughts of finishing his bath and going back to the castle were washed away as easily as soap suds. It was impossible to think of anything else when Tallant was in his immediate vicinity, nevermind when Tallant was naked.

Growing up, a silly boy whose days were filled with books, ink, and fanciful daydreams, Cecil had been enamored—infatuated, even—with elves, elven culture, the way they bonded so strongly, took any and all bonds so seriously. Not that humans didn't. But no elf would leave orphans to fend for themselves. Would reject someone out of hand for their station. Would never think of turning away someone fate had dictated they should pull in close.

Reality, of course, was that elves were people, shockingly. And while some things might be more taboo in elvish culture than in human, the reverse was also true. Still, when it felt like he and Irene had had no one but each other, he hadn't been able to resist the bond tattoos. They'd always been his favorite bit of elven culture, the bold markings that told the whole world the nature of a relationship between two people without any words needing to be said. For a painfully shy boy who'd been—and still was—terrible with words, the idea had been irresistible.

Seeing Tallant for the first time had been a punch in the gut. Not the kind that left you doubled over gasping and wheezing in pain, but the kind that had you on the ground curled up in a ball, tears streaming down your face as you tried desperately to remember how to breathe.

Tallant was fanciful daydreams brought to life, but a thousand times better.

And Cecil would never, in a thousand years, even *think* of admitting that. His brother and Irene were already unbearable about it, since they remembered far too well how stupid he'd been as a boy, and Tallant needed no encouragement in being a smug, smirking bastard.

"Stop scowling," Tallant said as he waded into the water and right up into Cecil's space, just like he'd been doing almost right from the start. He didn't give Cecil a chance to reply, just took his mouth in one of those breathtaking kisses that had been Cecil's undoing right from the start.

What was he supposed to have done, when a beautiful elf had come appearing out of nowhere to help rescue the castle and court him ardently. Resist? He was stubborn, not stupid.

Cecil went easily when Tallant all but dragged him to the bank and pushed him down into the soft, sun-warmed grass. From his throat dangled the necklace Cecil had made him: a wooden locket carved with two wolves wrapped around each other, forming a perfect circle. Making it had taken him ages, especially since he'd had to start over more than once, his hands no longer what they'd once been after years of fighting dragons and other rough work.

It wasn't nearly as beautiful as it had been in his head, despite his best efforts, but Tallant insisted he loved it, and never took it off, so Cecil was content. Even if the nitwit had promptly gone and cut a piece of Cecil's hair to keep inside, like some maiden waiting for her sailor to return.

Tallant kissed him again, sending Cecil's thoughts scattering once and for all. He tasted like his ridiculously too-sweet tea, and also honey cakes, which meant somebody had been sneaking into the kitchens again, like the spoiled brat he was. "Stop cozening the cook into giving you treats ahead of schedule."

"Never," Tallant said breathlessly. "What's it take to cozen a treat from you?"

"Shut up," Cecil said, the words automatic, because they both knew all Tallant had to do was bat his eyes and Cecil would do whatever he asked. He took care of the matter himself by putting teeth to Tallant's throat, right where his pulse beat, which as always reduced Tallant to swearing in his native language.

"So who's having who?" Tallant asked when he had recovered slightly, though it turned into a moan as Cecil teasingly stroked his cock.

Cecil nibbled at his throat again, free hand teasing along soft skin, the occasional rope or patch of scar. "Phrasing is unclear. Does having you mean I fuck you, or does it mean you fuck me?"

That got him a hard, bitey kiss, and then Tallant put him on his hands and knees, folding over him, skin hot and slick with sweat already. "I've decided I'm fucking you."

"Oh, no, woe is me," Cecil said, but further remarks were forgotten as Tallant grinded against him. Anticipation sent shivers running through him, prickling his skin and making the back of neck tangle.

Slick fingers pushed inside him, two of them, twisting and crooking in that way guaranteed to make Cecil moan. Sometimes it took his breath away how quickly he'd gone from too shy to even take a kiss without prompting, to being overwhelmed by a single blowjob, to begging loudly to be fucked right there in the middle of the woods where anyone could chance upon them. "Get to it, you useless elf."

Tallant chuckled, low and smug. "You're moaning far too much for me to be useless." But he withdrew his fingers and replaced them with his cock, sending Cecil into all new levels of moaning and whimpering. When he was fully seated, he plastered himself to Cecil's back again and bit the back of his neck, leaving Cecil swearing. "I do like when you're desperate for me, kel."

Lover. But it also carried softer meanings, along the lines of 'darling' and 'sweetheart'. Cecil had never thought himself much for ridiculous endearments, but there was little point in denying he melted every time Tallant called him that. He'd seemed to know all of Cecil's weaknesses right from the start, when even

Cecil hadn't known them. "Tallant. Damn it."

Chuckling again, Tallant rose back up and finally started to fuck him properly, pulling out and slamming back in, setting up a fast, hard pace that whited out the world around them, reduced it to just the two of them, the feel of Tallant's hands at his hips, his cock sinking deep, the sweat dripping into his eyes and the grass that would leave stains on his palms and knees.

Tallant eventually reached around and grabbed his cock, and a couple of rough, slick strokes was all it took to send Cecil screaming over the edge. He was still recovering when Tallant sank in deep one last time and wrapped tightly around him as he came.

They collapsed in a sweaty, stick pile, panting heavily for several minutes before finally disentangling. "So did you come out here for some other purpose?"

"Nope," Tallant said. "I was just hoping to catch you bathing, and enjoy myself without interruption."

"Shameless." Cecil dragged himself to a sitting position, and slapped Tallant playfully on the stomach. "Now I have to bathe all over again."

"What if I'm not done with you?" Tallant asked with a pout.

"You had me this morning and just now. I think you're done with me for a bit," Cecil said with a laugh, and waded back into the stream—and bellowing in outrage when he was tackled from behind, dragged into the icy water while Bite and Raze continued to watch indolently from the bank.

At My Side

THE ROYAL INQUISITOR

Esmour yawned as he walked through the rapidly descending dark, people around him hastening their steps to get back to their warm homes before night took over and all the trouble came out. By day, the royal capital was usually a marvelous place to be, but by night even the royal guards, and Teigh's dedicated shadow workings via their inquisitors, could only do so much.

He yawned a second time barely before finishing the first one, so hard his eyes watered and he ran out of breath for a moment—and then went careening to the ground as someone's shoulder slammed into him. "Damn it," he muttered, picking himself up and checking that he hadn't just landed in a puddle of piss or worse.

"You'll watch your language," said a frigid voice.

Esmour stilled, then slowly dragged his eyes up, starring at the finely dressed man before him. A noble, but not one Esmour knew. There were so many titled, and he spent so much time on his duties, that he doubted he'd ever learn them all. Teigh assured him he didn't need to, but given all Esmour *did* have memorized, it seemed silly he couldn't keep up with all the fops and baubles of court. On the other hand, if he didn't need to know their name, that was all to the good, because nobody wanted the Deputy Chief Inquisitor to know them.

"Well?" the man said. "What have you to say for yourself?"

For a moment, Esmour considered the mature route: tell the man who he was, who his lover was, and why it would probably be unwise to piss him off. But he'd spent most of his life being trod upon by arrogant, mean-hearted bastards like this. Kicked, shoved aside, literally stepped on. Spit on, backhanded. He'd had friends beaten, raped, and left to bleed out in the gutters.

So instead he slipped into the familiar 'peasant' accent he'd grown up with, before he'd learned how to speak 'properly' in various languages. "'Twas you what ran into me, milord."

That got him the backhand he expected, the man's ring slicing into his cheek, leaving a cut that would scar if not properly tended. "Watch your tongue. Be on your way before I decided to summon the guards to deal with you."

Esmour smiled, and the man at least had enough sense to recoil slightly. "Accidents happen on crowded streets. Bit of patience and kindness wouldn't have hurt you none. But being a mean, rude bastard just because you can be—that will hurt you. G'evening, milord." Esmour strode on while the man was still sputtering, vanishing easily into the crowd even as the man started bellowing for guards. Who would only be greatly annoyed that they were being disturbed simply because someone had been rude.

He reached the royal castle a short time later, slipping through a side gate with a smile and wave at the guards as they let him through. He stole into the kitchens briefly to nick a couple of pies, taking a playful swat from the head chef with good grace and a kiss to her cheek.

They were stuffed full with hen and vegetables, dripping gravy and burning the roof of his mouth. He finished the last couple of bites as he reached his chambers, and was greeted by a familiar chuckle. "Sometimes I think you only love me for the access to the royal kitchens."

Esmour grinned and licked the last remaining bits of gravy from his thumb. "It's a perk."

"Somehow—" Teigh broke off, a scowl overtaking his face. "Who hit you?" He dropped the papers he was holding and strode across the room, spurs ringing with every hard step, and took gentle hold of Esmour's face. "Only a jeweled ring could cut like that. Tell me who did it."

Esmour tugged free of his grip. "Leave off,

noble prince. I have the matter well in hand. Anyway, I've no idea who the man was. He's not a face I've seen before, but that doesn't mean much. Given your brother has returned today, however, I'm sure I'll see him again before the night is out. Now do I get a kiss, or are you just going to keep scowling?"

"I'm going to attend that cut on your cheek," Teigh said, not quite growling the words as he took hold of Esmour's wrist and dragged him back across the room, shoving him into the chair at his table before going to fetch the healer's kit he always kept in the room.

Esmour rolled his eyes. "It's barely a scratch."

"You know very well it's worse than that." Teigh unrolled the kit on his table, shoving papers carelessly out of the way, and grasped Esmour's chin to look the cut over critically. "I really want someone to suffer for this."

"For a simple backhand?" Esmour scoffed. "I told you, I have the matter well in hand. I know how to deal with spoiled brat nobles." He fluttered his lashes. "Does my prince no longer find me appealing, without my pretty face?"

That got exactly the reaction he'd been hoping for: dragged out of the chair and practically thrown right across the table, sending papers scattering everywhere as Teigh settled between his spread thighs and kissed him until they were both gasping for breath.

"You're a brat," Teigh finally said, barely withdrawing enough to get the words out.

Esmour kissed his nose. "I wanted a kiss, damn it."

"That cut needs tending."

"And you can tend it all you like now I've gotten my kiss."

Teigh sighed and dragged him back off the table, looking over the mess he'd made. "You certainly know how to get your way."

"I am the King's Lymer," Esmour replied with a smile, and resumed his seat when Teigh pointed, tilting his head so Teigh could fuss over the cut as he wanted.

Gentle fingers rubbed a sweet-smelling salve over the cut. "That reminds me of something I wanted to discuss with you."

Esmour's good mood vanished as the suddenly serious tone struck him. "What?"

"By the gods, Esmour, it's nothing bad!" Teigh tugged him to his feet and brushed a soft kiss across his mouth. "You are mine. That will never change if I have anything to say about it."

"Sorry," Esmour said. "Despite everything, I still sometimes fear I'll wake up cold and alone in an alleyway, all of this a dream."

"You're my dream come true, poet," Teigh replied, wrapping him up close and kissing him deeply. "Which is what I wanted to talk to you about."

Esmour gave him a look. "You want to

discuss my being a dream?"

"Stop being a brat!" Teigh shook him gently. "No, I want to discuss the fact you're mine. And my father's precious Lymer. You've served him now for a little over four years, and have been *mine*, not Amabel's or anyone else's, for more than a year."

"You don't usually ramble this much."

Teigh groaned. "You're right, I don't. But in my defense you're the only person in the world who makes me nervous."

"That's stupid."

"Shut up and let me talk!" Teigh pinched him. "How would you feel, King's Lymer, about being His Majesty's son-in-law as well?"

Esmour stared blankly. "How in the world would I be his son-in-law? I'd have to marry—" His eyes snapped open wide. "You can't mean—are you asking me—"

"To marry me, yes, although in my head I was a lot more elegant and intelligent about it." Teigh sighed. "Why do you look like you swallowed a frog?"

"Because four years ago I slept on the streets and stole to survive, and one year ago I was in penance bracelets, and now you want me to *marry into the royal family.*" He sat down before he fell down, swallowing the sudden lump in his throat, too many thoughts and emotions swirling through his head for any single one to really latch on properly.

Teigh knelt in front of him, covering Esmour's hands with his own. "Surely you knew this is where our path would eventually lead."

Esmour gave him a look. "You must be joking. It is one thing for a prince to take some tarted-up thief for a lover. Quite another to *marry* him. Your father—"

"Has already given his permission," Teigh said quietly.

"Oh." Esmour stared at their joined hands, hating that his trembled but unable to help it. He still couldn't believe he was an earl most days, and now Teigh wanted to make him a prince?

Teigh's hands tensed, and withdrew slightly. "You don't have to say yes, if the idea troubles you."

Esmour laughed shakily and grabbed his hands back. "It doesn't trouble me, not the way you clearly think. It's intimidating, and you could do a thousand times better than—"

"No, I couldn't," Teigh said, with all the fierceness that made him such an excellent Chief Royal Inquisitor. "You loved me when I was a merchant. You loved me when I betrayed you. You're steadfast and true, and lovely inside and out. There is no better person in this whole kingdom, and I want you at my side, officially and forever."

Tears stung Esmour's eyes. "You know that's all I ever wanted, be you merchant or prince or if tomorrow we both woke up gutter rats. Of course I'll marry you, Teigh."

Teigh rose and dragged him out of the chair and into his arms, kissing him ravenously, possessively, before shoving-guiding him over to the bed and making quick work of their clothes. Normally Teigh loved to take his time, take Esmour apart piece by piece, until he was left wrung-out and practically melted.

But right then his legendary patience was nowhere to be found, and it was only moments before he spread Esmour wide and sank into him, fucking him with rough, eager strokes that had Esmour clinging for dear life, his moans filling the room.

He came a short time later, spilling between them as Teigh fucked him a last few times before coming deep inside him, face buried in Esmour's throat.

When they could move again, sweat cooling on Esmour's skin and making him slightly chilly, Teigh rolled off him and sprawled across the bed. "There's a bath for you, by the way."

Esmour glanced over toward the fire place, where sure enough, a bath was still steaming gently. "Thank you. Though I'm not sure I can move now."

Teigh laughed and helped him up, then ushered him into the water and, despite Esmour's protests, set to washing him.

Nearly an hour later, and after Teigh had made liberal use of Esmour's mouth, they were finally dressed and ready for dinner. Teigh kissed him gently, mindful of Esmour's poor, well-used lips, and went over to his wardrobe. He came back with something tucked into his fist, and uncurled his fingers one by one to reveal a simple, but handsome ring: three small emeralds set in gleaming gold.

Esmour swallowed and offered his left hand, watching as Teigh slid the ring into place, noting belatedly that he already wore a matching ring, though it had glittering yellow diamonds instead of emeralds. "Engaged to a prince. If my old crew could see me now, they'd not believe it." He smiled and kissed the corner of Teigh's mouth. "Take me to dinner, Highness."

Teigh's eyes glittered. "Yes, Highness."

"Stop that!" Esmour was still laughing, torn between elation and terror, as they headed down the hallway. It faded as they neared the great hall, and a familiar figure caught his gaze.

The man's eyes widened. "You! What are *you* doing here?"

Teigh's brows shot up into his hairline. "I beg your pardon, Lord Marsten?"

Marsten seemed to realize something was amiss. "Beg pardon, Your Highness, but I met this man a short time ago on the streets. He was dressed quite common, and had no manners to speak of."

"So what explains your lack of manners?" Teigh asked, in a voice that had sent many a soldier and inquisitor looking desperately for escape routes. "I forget, though, that you've been out of the country for quite some time. I'm sure that explains much of your… misunderstanding. Let me clear things up for you. Lord Marsten, this is Lord Esmour Locke, Earl of Halfnight, King's Lymer, Deputy Chief Inquisitor, and as of an hour ago, my betrothed. Esmour, this is Lord Hannigan Marsten, Marquis of Grace. If you are my father's Lymer, he is my father's trash collector. Isn't that right, my lord?"

Marsten looked as though he'd been slapped, or like he was about to toss up his stomach, but he gave a terse nod and said, "Just so, Your Highness. I apologize for my behavior, Lord Locke. Congratulations on your engagement." He didn't wait for their replies, simply fled the scene against all protocol.

Esmour cast Teigh a look. "I told you I had the matter well in hand."

"I'm not just going to simply stand by and let some rude upstart treat you that way," Teigh said. "You're far too nice to all these rude bastards. He's lucky I was in too good a mood to give him what he really deserves."

"Down, sweet prince, my honor has been thoroughly defended. I'd much rather go show off my ring."

Teigh grinned. "Steal all the attention from my brother?"

"That is not what I said."

"But it is what I'm going to do," Teigh said, offering his arm, smiling unrepentantly as he led them into the crowded hall.

Fin

About the Author

Megan is a long-time resident of queer romance, and keeps herself busy reading and writing it. She is often accused of fluff and nonsense. When she's not involved in writing, she likes to cook, harass her wife and cats, or watch movies. She loves to hear from readers, and can be found all over the internet.

meganderr.com
patreon.com/meganderr
pillowfort.io/maderr
meganderr.blogspot.com
facebook.com/meganaprilderr
meganaderr@gmail.com
@meganaderr

www.ingramcontent.com/pod-product-compliance
Ingram Content Group UK Ltd.
Pitfield, Milton Keynes, MK11 3LW, UK
UKHW041954190726
13854UKWH00005B/1974

9 798633 154672